A Crate Full of Lemons

A Crate Full of Lemons

A Novel

Lloyd Gordon

First Edition
2014

Printed in the United States of America.

ISBN-13: 978-1499503937
ISBN-10: 1499503938

Cover Photography: © Helena Goessens Photography

Seeing your child for the first time, your life changes.

*You know love, you know the fear of not succeeding,
and you make a heart-beating commitment to really try.*

To those few I love.

CHAPTER ONE
Snow

I remember it looked like snow.

Convocation Hall was jammed. There was a student in every single seat. Standing would never be allowed. At Stanton Academy, smack in the middle of pristine Boston, appearances were paramount.

Headmaster Arthur Winn stood at the podium. He was dressed in a perfect black suit—made just a tad incongruous by his choice of a bright-red sweater vest and an orange tie.

Orange I could understand. We were the Stanton Tigers, and orange was our school color.

The red sweater vest demanded a further explanation.

A lot of things, I've learned in life, demand further explanation. All the things that were going to happen to my brother and to me—to our family—to our friends—they all demanded further explanation. That it would all somehow culminate in me driving a van full of money that belonged to other people toward a border crossing in Laredo would—I think—demand further explanation most of all.

All that will come in time.

But at that particular time—sitting in Convocation Hall—my brain began to mentally stray. It was gray outside—yet a kind of welcoming gray. It wasn't cold, but there was that definite feeling in the air—of impending snow.

I remembered that about six weeks ago, we were home for Sunday dinner, and my mother looked out the window into our back yard and said, "Boys, it looks like snow."

My brother Todd—sometimes called Double-D—took out his iPhone and pronounced, "No snow today, Mom. It's going to be forty degrees and sunny."

I'm Tim Shaw. My brother Todd and I are identical twins.

But we didn't look that much alike. We couldn't trick people. I was an inch taller, and, even though we both had blond hair, Todd's hair was a much darker blond and it was really, really thick.

Todd had a bigger laugh.

He laughed at my mother and held up the phone to show her the weather icon that proclaimed sunny skies.

"It's going to snow," my mother rejoined.

An hour later we were hit with a freak September snow squall. Less than an inch piled up before it stopped. But that was enough for my mother. As she was serving a hearty beef-stew dinner, she looked at Todd and said with a big smile, "It still looks like snow."

We laughed and grabbed homemade hot rolls to dunk into our stew.

That was before.

Before seasons had a chance to end. Before new seasons had a chance to begin.

My mother would never see another season. And neither would my father.

My dad, Timothy Shaw, Sr., graduated from Stanford with a degree in applied mathematics and then got his PhD at MIT in theoretical calculus.

At MIT, he met a fellow math whiz, Marion Shaw. That's not a mistake. My father, Tim Shaw, met a girl named Marion Shaw, no relation.

They went out. They went steady. They moved in together. They got married after graduation.

My mother could have called herself Marion Shaw Shaw, but simply went with one surname.

"Which Shaw do you use?" I asked my mom once.

"Oh, that depends," she said.

"On what?"

"On what your father gets me for my birthday."

Anyway, Mom never got a job that required her math skills. She worked in a bakery after she finished at MIT. Imagine that? It started out as a favor to a friend's mother and was supposed to last a week. But Mom discovered that she loved baking.

My dad, meanwhile, pounced on his degrees and became an actuary with New England Mutual of Boston. He worked long hours. Hard hours. He knew everything there was to know. More importantly, he knew what he was supposed to know and what he didn't know—he threw himself at it until he knew it.

The result of it all was promotion after promotion.

The result of it all was a fortune.

The result of it all was Mom and Dad dying on a cold October afternoon.

Dad had become enamored of flying. I have no idea why. He wasn't a sportsman. He wasn't an adventurer. He drove a Volvo. A gray Volvo with a gray interior.

But somehow, somewhere along the line, he got a bug about small planes. Maybe it was the math involved. The theory of lift. Thrust and drag and gravity and curved wings.

He knew how a plane flew. He understood the physics.

But, why did he buy an old plane? A Cessna 172 that had been left outside under a huge tarp on the tarmac at a very small airport in Norwood. My father heard about the plane through a colleague. There was something about the idea of buying an old plane and taking it apart and fixing all the pieces and putting it all back together that made his eyes shine more than I had ever seen.

It took him more than two years to get it ready. He did all of the work himself. He took mechanic classes. He bought equipment. He cleaned, he sanded, he polished, he re-built—he gave it everything he had.

He took flying lessons while all this was going on and got his pilot's license well before the plane was finished.

What he didn't know, of course, was that the new gascolater fuel-bowl assembly he bought was actually a refurbished gascolater fuel-bowl assembly. He could have found an old one and refurbished it himself, and it would have been better than new. But, he reasoned, buying a new one would save him at least a week's worth of work—and he wanted to fly Mom up north to Vermont to our ski house. Not to ski. But to see the foliage from the air.

"I want you to see the colors like you've never seen them before," he told Mom.

She kissed him—passionately—on the mouth—right in front of us. I'd never seen Mom and Dad kiss like that.

Buying the gascolater fuel-bowl assembly would save him a critical week. A week in autumn when the foliage would peak. The next week after that would be too late.

We said goodbye to Mom and Dad on a Sunday, just before we returned to our dorm at Stanton Academy.

On Monday, while Todd and I were in our Calculus III class, going over equations that Sir Isaac Newton had generated, my dad and mom took off. Dad pointed the plane toward Vermont. Mom had her new digital Nikon at the ready.

Sir Isaac, of course, is famous for his laws of motion.

He never made any pronouncements about faultily refurbished gascolater fuel-bowl assemblies, but I'm sure he would have appreciated the forces of wind, resistance and gravity and what they do to a small plane that has suddenly stalled in mid-air.

There was some solace in the fact that the plane didn't explode on impact. Maybe all the fuel had leaked out? At least the bodies weren't burnt. At least Mom and Dad were spared that indignity.

Headmaster Winn!

Headmaster Winn had been talking about us. About our loss. About how it was also the school's loss. The Stanton Academy family's loss.

As was the tradition at Stanton, a scholarship fund had been set up for Todd and myself—to ensure that our graduation would be guaranteed. Of course we didn't need the scholarship. What dad had left in his checking account alone was guarantee enough that we would graduate from Stanton, as well as any college we attended.

Headmaster Winn knew this as well. The scholarship offer was simply a gesture. But it was a heartfelt gesture, and Todd and I appreciated it.

The convocation was over.

Everyone yelled, "Thank you, Mr. Winn. We're all Winners!"

Okay, it's dorky. But it's sort of fun at the same time.

We stood, as usual, to sing "Hymn to Stanton."

Then we filtered outside and went our various ways. Todd had an English class and I had to go back to my dorm room to prepare a paper on differential calculus.

I was walking by myself, along a narrow little gravel path that wended among some dogwoods.

I was thinking about Mom and Dad. The foliage. The changing seasons. Our changing lives. I had my hands in my pockets because it was getting colder.

It started to snow.

I stopped for a brief moment and looked straight up at the swirling flakes—flying and flitting and jumping on air currents.

I smiled and started walking again.

"Thanks, Mom," I whispered to myself.

CHAPTER TWO
Lemons

Uncle Elliot had spoken at the funeral.

Then Uncle Elliot had spoken to us.

"It's all because of survivor's insurance," Uncle Elliot said.

"What do you mean, Uncle Elliot?" I asked.

"Tim, my brother, your father, and I had survivor's insurance. On each other. If one of us dies, the other one gets all the trust money. All the savings. Everything."

I knew what he was saying, but I simply couldn't get my brain to accept it.

"Everything is mine now," Uncle Elliot said.

"But—"

Todd started to speak and then stopped.

"But," I took up, "you're going to give it to us, right?"

"No. I'm not going to give it to you. It's not your money. It's my money."

I should have been mad. Maybe it was the simple math involved. I just didn't get mad. It was just—just the last part of losing Mom and Dad.

Todd was in near shock. It wasn't the money that shocked him. It was Uncle Elliot.

It wasn't that we were poor. Uncle Elliot pointed out that we could sell our city house and our Vermont house and clear about six million dollars.

We could regroup.

But—he was our uncle. He had never married and he had no children. He was supposed to look at us as if we were his kids. That had to be what my father had intended.

We were the kids Uncle Elliot took to Fenway. Now he took us to the cleaners.

I'll give Uncle Elliot credit for one thing. Sort of. He didn't run away. He moved into our house in the Back Bay.

For four days.

He did have the decency to leave a note.

"I have things to attend to."

Six words.

Six words to explain to his orphaned nephews, the only relatives he had, and he being the only relative we had, why he wouldn't be with us any more.

Uncle Elliot was gone.

We were alone.

We had no relatives left.

We had no legal guardian.

We looked at each other and decided that we liked this situation just fine.

We wouldn't tell anyone. We wouldn't seek legal recourse.

We didn't need help.

CHAPTER THREE
Marisol

When I met Marisol, I was old enough to appreciate her, but too young to do anything about it.

Marisol was the most vibrant woman I had ever seen.

She looked taller than she was. Her waist was incredibly slim. Her sensuous neck accented her dark chestnut hair that fell down just beyond her shoulders. She had a habit of twisting her long exotic fingers through her hair when she spoke. Her face was more than perfect. Her lips made men believe that life was worth living.

When she walked into the front entry of our dorm that first time, and she took off her long elegant black-leather coat—to reveal a figure that would make grown men weep and vaporize teenage boys—I fell more madly than I would ever fall.

Her voice! A mild Spanish accent. A Mediterranean masterpiece of liquid passion. She was simply too elegant, too exotic, too other worldly. She was out of any league that I could only dream of being in. She played center field for the Red Sox, and I was a back-up catcher for the single-A affiliate in Des Moines.

She said she needed to find the office of Elmore Duncan—Professor Duncan, head of the math department.

Maybe this is his wife? No. The Dunk was a buffoon—aside from prodigious math skills—and he could never ever land a babe like this.

Todd, thinking on his feet a little quicker than I was, offered to escort her to the math department.

"I'll go with you," I blurted out.

"No," Todd said, "you have to study."

"No," I said, my voice raising in panic, "I have to see the Dunk—Professor Duncan, I mean. He's giving me an extra-credit assignment."

Todd didn't have a comeback.

"I don't need extra credit," I said to Marisol, happy that my brain was functioning again, at least on a standby basis. "I have a hundred-and-five average, of course. But one never knows what the future might bring—say in a year or so."

"That," Marisol said, "is a very mature thing to think."

Mature. She thought of me as mature.

With the Shaw twins flanking her, we walked this beauty of beauties across the green to the math department.

Where was my brain? Marisol was speaking and I almost didn't catch what she had said.

She was asking us about Carlos Herrara.

Carlos was a year behind us. We knew him. He was on the math team and was, quite frankly, almost as good as we were. Almost.

"Does Carlos like it here at this school?"

"Sure," I said.

"Why do you ask?" Todd added.

"It's just that his phone calls are always so—quick. He never gives me any of the details. But I know he likes his math. So I thought I'd start with the Dun—I mean with Professor Duncan."

"Are you Carlos' mother?" I asked.

Her eyes widened—if that were possible.

"Of course I am the mother of Carlos. Didn't you know that? I know that Stanton Academy isn't the most—what is your word?—diverse—of schools. And I don't care. But how many Spanish students are there?"

None with a supermodel mother, I heard myself saying. Luckily, I said it silently.

"Oh—" is what I said.

"Oh—" Todd echoed.

"I am from Barcelona. Barcelona is the beauty of my country. My Carlos was born here. He can be president. But I can't."

"Oh, you can be anything you want to be," I silently prayed.

Further talk would have been as pointless as impossible.

We escorted Marisol to the math department and then Todd and I slinked away,

But math would bring us back to Marisol.

Todd and I had inherited our parents' love and understanding of all forms of math. To us, math was the same as breathing.

We played sports at Stanton—simply because it was required. Football, Indoor Track, Lacrosse. We weren't good at all.

We thrived on the Math Team.

Sunday afternoons in some dark small auditorium where not even parents bothered to attend.

We never scored a touchdown, won a race or shot a goal.

But put us in one of those dark small auditoriums where not even parents bothered to attend—and we came home with the trophy each and every time.

We found ourselves so advanced in math, that Mr. Duncan put Todd and me—along with Carlos—in charge of creating a system of education modeled on Kahn Academy. We came up with Stanton Online. Over the course of a year we recorded two hundred and thirty lessons about algebra, geometry, trigonometry and calculus.

Marisol was so happy that we had included Carlos in our project that she started visiting every week or so and brought "care packages." Cookies. Brownies. All manner of delicious things.

We'd be in our room, and down the hall we could hear that elegant, raspy accent calling our names.

The blood shot everywhere in our bodies.

Marisol always gave each of us a great big hug and asked how we were doing.

We knew that she meant how were we doing since our parents had died, but we pretended that we thought she meant how were we doing in school.

So it still came as a huge surprise one day in math class when Carlos sort of blurted out—right in front of Professor Duncan and all the kids, "Mom wants you guys to come and live with us."

CHAPTER FOUR
A New Family

"What?" I asked Carlos. "What did you just say?"

"Mom wants you to come and live with us."

"With you and Marisol?" I heard myself say. Then I added a bit weakly. "I mean your mom."

So the gist of it was this.

Carlos' mom—the enchanting Marisol—thought we shouldn't be on our own. We were old enough to take care of ourselves, but she thought that we needed a family.

"So, you guys want to move in or what?" Carlos asked.

"Let us think about it," Todd managed to say.

We didn't have math team that day after school, so Todd and I decided to walk home. It would take us about a half hour. We'd do this when we needed to talk.

"I don't know if I like the idea," Todd said. "You know. We're not charity cases."

"Oh, no. Marisol wouldn't mean that."

"*Marisol*? You've got to be kidding. She's like fifty."

"She is not," I said. "I bet she's thirty-two. And what difference does it make? Just look at her. She could be a hundred and thirty-two and I wouldn't mind!"

Todd stopped walking.

"Tim. Listen to yourself."

"Okay," I said. "You can't blame a guy for lust, can you? So?"

"So, what?"

"Should we move in with them?"

"Let's talk about it after dinner."

We always did a good job of cleaning up. Which is funny because cleaning becomes sort of important later on in this story. We cleaned up because of Mom. Her house was her castle. To make our decision, we did what both Mom and Dad would have done. We made a list of reasons to decline the offer and reasons to accept the offer.

"We have to give each item a point value and then add it all up," I said.

Todd looked over the list.

"Item one to accept the offer: 'Marisol.' I'd say that's worth a thousand points."

"No need to add up the rest," I said.

"You can't argue with math," Todd said.

CHAPTER FIVE
The Deal

"I was so very happy to get your note," Marisol Herrara said when she opened the door to greet us. "I'm so very happy that you've accepted our offer."

Over dinner, we brought up the question of rent.

"I will not hear of it. It is insulting to me. You are my guests."

"Mrs. Herrara," Todd said. "The last thing we'd ever want to do—and never would do—is insult you."

"Double-D is right," I blurted out.

"What?" she said. "What is this Double-D?"

"That's me," Todd said. "my name ends with double D."

"That is very—adorable," Marisol said, smiling at Todd.

"The thing of it is," I said, "is that we want to be responsible for our own lives. We want to preserve our autonomy."

"Autonomy—" began Carlos.

"I know what autonomy means, my Carlos," Marisol said. "And the last thing I would ever want to do would be to—diminish—anyone's precious autonomy."

She gave us a look that would make a charging bull slam to a sudden stop.

"So. How about ten thousand dollars a month?" Todd said.

Oh, no. The look. Five bulls. Ten bulls. Slammed to a sudden stop in the sand of a silent arena.

"Boys," Marisol said, "you have to have standards. You cannot buy the life you live with money. I will accept one thousand dollars a month. For that, you each get your own room, use of the entire house, and all meals. I expect that we live here as a family—I don't expect you to think of me as your—family—you know, I am not replacing anyone—but I expect you to act like we are together in all of this. You're not boarders. And you're not my children. But we will act like a family. A new sort of family. Is that—agreeable—to you?"

"Yes," Todd said.

"Yes," I said.

"Fine. You should move in this weekend. You can pay for your own moving truck."

CHAPTER SIX
Rich Boys

Six million dollars is *not* a lot of money.

The first thing that had to be done was to legally make Marisol what they call a custodial guardian. Dad's lawyer set this up. State law required that we be with an adult until we were eighteen. Marisol agreed to be this adult and we signed papers to that effect. She wasn't our legal guardian. She wasn't responsible for our finances. She was the person in the house who we said we'd call if we were going to be late for dinner.

Once that was finalized, we sold our two houses. We went to our bank—Boston United Savings Bank on Tremont Street—and we met with Sheldon Crummins, Vice President of Investments. Shel, as he insisted we call him, took care of everything.

"I knew your father very well," Shel said. "I don't understand at all why he and your Uncle Elliott entered into that survivor's agreement. There were so many other ways to handle things. So many other protections that could have easily been done. But, here we are."

"Here we are," I said, thinking we were lucky to be in such good hands.

We signed as many papers as he could put on his desk in an hour.

"Can we sign these?" I asked, "even though we're not eighteen yet?"

"Yes," Shel said. "The first one is what's called a pro-tem power-of-attorney. It covers all bases, but just for these particular transactions."

Shel quickly arranged for a bank-appointed trustee to sell both houses. It only took a week! Amazing. But these were prime properties in vaunted locations.

We cleared, all together, six million, two hundred and eighty-five thousand, one hundred and nineteen dollars and eleven cents.

It didn't make things even with what Uncle Elliot did.

But it put us in a new game that we could play well.

CHAPTER SEVEN
Mom

We settled into our life in Marisol's elegant home on Beacon Hill.

We threw ourselves into school as usual—but we found ourselves coming home every weekend, just for the food. It was a little spicier than we were accustomed to, but we quickly grew to really love it.

The school year ended and the four of us took a trip to California—to Santa Monica. It was a surprise trip. For no reason. Marisol said she just needed a change and that she'd like to go to the beach there.

I admit that my first thought was of getting to see Marisol in a bikini.

We rented a condo right on the beach—along a picturesque narrow paved walkway that runs all along the edge of the beach up about a hundred yards from the water.

It was a good rest.

About three weeks into it, there was a day when it rained. We hadn't been doing all that much—but, still, there's something so comforting about a day of rain that lets you do nothing—and do it without any guilt.

The rain eased off to a mist by about three in the afternoon and Todd wanted to go for a run along the beach.

Todd was upstairs—we could hear him rummaging around for something. We heard his voice calling out.

"Mom. Did you see my Nike sneakers?"

"Check the laundry room," she offered.

"Thanks," Todd called out.

A minute later we heard, "Got 'em."

Todd came bounding down the stairs and stopped dead when he saw Marisol.

"Why are you crying?" he asked her.

Carlos and I turned our gaze toward her.

She leaned forward and put her face into her hands. She cried louder and louder.

The two of us looked at Carlos, who could only shrug. He hadn't a clue.

Todd went to Marisol and put his hand out and gently touched her shoulder.

"What is it?" he asked.

After a moment, she looked up at us.

"I shouldn't have come here," she said. "It was a mistake. It was a stupid, stupid mistake. I was an idiot to come here."

"Please, Mrs. Herrara," I said, "please tell us what's wrong."

"Don't call me Mrs. Herrara," she said.

"Sorry," I said. "Okay. What's wrong—Marisol?"

"And don't call me Marisol either."

I looked at her. I said nothing.

She stood and went to the window and looked out toward the water. After a full minute—a full minute of silence that felt long enough for the earth to have made one trip around the sun—she turned back to us and spoke.

"This place. This beach. This ocean. I thought that coming here—after fourteen years—would be a way to find some peace. But that was a big, big mistake."

"You've been here before, Mom?" Carlos asked.

"Yes," she said. "Fourteen years ago."

She looked at Carlos and then she added, "With you and your brother."

We were rocked to stillness.

No one moved. No one spoke.

Marisol walked to Carlos and put her hands up to his face.

"Forgive me, Carlos. Forgive me, my Carlos. Please, please—find it in your heart to forgive me."

"I don't understand," Carlos said.

"Neither do I," Marisol replied. "Neither do I."

She wiped her eyes and she turned to look out to the water. With her back to us, she started telling a story.

"You had a brother," she said. "A baby brother. You were two-and-a-half and he was just a year old. His name was Martinez. He was named after your father. You, Carlos, were named after my father. We had come here, the four of us, because my husband, Martinez, wanted to buy a farm along the coast. He wanted to grow tomatoes. He was going to be very rich. And we were going to be very happy."

"But, wait," Carlos said. "You told me that my father was a shop owner. That you were only married for three weeks when he suddenly died."

"A lie, my Carlos. The first of many lies. No, your father and I had been married for four years when we came here to look for land for growing tomatoes.

"Every day, my husband Martinez would go out and look at land and talk to people. I and my sons would have a nice breakfast out on the little patio in front of the house and then we would go to the beach for the day.

"We'd sit on a blanket and make sandcastles. Each of you had a little bucket and a little shovel. But the sand near our blanket was very dry. Even with rain on the way, it was very dry. So we went down to the ocean to dig up mud and to use that mud to make a castle.

"I got very much into making the castle. I was a little bit bored, I guess, with two young boys. You don't know how it is yet. But when you have young children, your life just goes away. They consume you. So there I was at the water's edge digging up mud and making a castle any princess would love. Or prince. It had walls and a moat and it had three towers. One tower for each of us, I remember saying.

"I was sitting in the mud—my legs were covered in mud—and I was reaching up to put a seashell on top of one of the towers. You, Carlos, cried out and clapped your hands. I turned to see the reaction of Martinez.

"He wasn't there.

"My son. My boy. My Martinez. He wasn't there.

"Of course I jumped up and looked around—expecting to see him a few feet away. He was just a year old. He couldn't walk far.

"My heart was trying to kill me. I looked around and around. I spun around over and over. I stopped and called his name.

"Martinez! Martinez! Martinez!

"There was no one on that beach but us. I fell to my knees and looked out at the waves crashing into the shore. I put my hands up to my head and squeezed my skull from both sides.

"*Martinez!*

"I jumped up and grabbed you and ran up and down along the water's edge. Then I turned and ran up away from the water toward our house. There were no cell phones. I had to call for help. I had to have help. I must have help. To find Martinez."

Marisol turned and looked at us full in the face.

She wasn't crying.

She wasn't frantic.

She put her hands up to her skull and squeezed from both sides,

"He was gone. He must have taken a couple of steps—just a couple of steps while I was building the tower to the castle—and gone into the water a bit. A wave. A wave must have knocked him over and the undertow must have swept him out to sea. He was never found. My little Martinez rests in the ocean. For fourteen years, my little Martinez has rested in the ocean."

"Why didn't you ever tell me, Mom?" Carlos asked.

"I was so ashamed. It was all my fault. I'm the reason you're all alone, my Carlos. Your father, my husband Martinez, left us the moment he found out what had happened. He slapped me once across the face and called me a murderer. Then he was gone. Gone to I don't know where. He left me—which I could understand. But he also left you—Carlos. And that's why I couldn't tell you what happened. Because of me, you don't have a brother. Because of me, you don't have a father."

I opened my mouth to speak and said the first really intelligent thing I had ever said in my life.

"It's not your fault."

Marisol started to object, but I wouldn't let her speak.

"It wasn't your fault. It happened in an instant. It was an accident. A terrible accident. It could happen to anyone. It does happen to people. How could it have been your fault? You're a wonderful mother. You're a wonderful person. You're just like my mom and dad. Was it my dad's fault that he bought a part that failed? Did he kill my mother? Of course not. It was an accident. It wasn't your fault. I don't know your husband, but he was wrong to leave you. It was unpardonable for him to leave you and to leave Carlos. He's the one who should be consumed by guilt. Forget him. He's not worth it. All we care about is you."

Carlos stepped forward and gave his mother a hug. Todd and I put our arms around them both—and the tears were tears we could bear.

In a moment, the sun came out and filled the room with hope.

"Let's go for a walk on the beach," Marisol said.

Without a second of hesitation, the four of us were outside and walking along the sand.

"Tim?" she said.

"Yes?" I replied.

"I don't want you to call me, Mrs. Herrara."

"Okay."

"And I don't want you to call me, Marisol."

"Okay."

"I want you to call me, Mom."

I didn't say anything. All I could think about was Mom and Dad in that plane. Dropping down out of the sky. Knowing they would never see us again.

"Of course we'll call you, Mom," Todd said.

"Of course we will," I echoed.

"Do you think your mom would mind?" she asked.

I said no. Todd nodded in agreement.

"We know who our mother is," I said. "And we know she loved us. And we know we loved her."

"And," Todd said, "we know that she would be happy with you looking over us."

"So," I said, "please don't be tormented anymore. It's okay to be sad. Todd and I know that. But—please stop being tormented. Mom."

"Tim's right, Mom."

Marisol turned to the ocean for a moment and looked out at the waves.

Then she turned back to us.

"It was good that we came here," she said.

The four of us continued our walk along the beach, treading on the soft sand, letting the sounds of the ocean overpower us with a sense of understanding.

CHAPTER EIGHT
Fast Forward

It seemed like every time we turned around, we were graduating from somewhere.

Todd and I finished Stanton at the top of our class. We both went to Harvard. It was, in fact, the only college we had applied to. That was, naturally, quite arrogant. But we were in a let-the-devil-take-the-hindmost kind of mood. As the Christmas season approached during our senior year—when we should have been filling out college applications—we found ourselves in the habit of doing as little as possible each and every day. The idea of Christmas without Mom and Dad became monumental. It was of course our second Christmas without them; but the first one had been just weeks after they had died and we were caught up in the rush of the turmoil and the funeral and the whole mess with Uncle Elliot.

So this Christmas—was the Christmas when it hit home for real.

Carlos, on the other hand, got this weird idea that he wanted to catch up with us in school. So at the beginning of his junior year, when Todd and I were seniors, Carlos went to Headmaster Winn and laid it on thick. He wanted to double up on classes. Mr. Winn would have nothing to do with it. But Carlos got his mother involved and, well, when Marisol Herrara showed up for a school meeting, the school never had a chance.

Carlos took extra classes. He took classes in person. He took classes online. He did independent study for three English classes—writing a one-act play, a collection of short stories and an epic poem about the Boston Red Sox that satisfied all requirements.

On graduation day—although he still had to take three classes that coming summer—he was on stage with all of us and got a blank diploma. But, and this is key to this story, while we were essentially staring at the ceiling, Carlos applied to Harvard on a "special-needs" basis. There is no such thing as a special-needs basis for application, but Carlos went to a dean at Harvard and talked his way in. He didn't take Marisol into the meeting with him; but she was there in the outer waiting area and when the dean came out to meet Carlos, Marisol stood as dramatically as only Marisol can, and she changed her stance and shook her hair from side to side and then took the dean's hand and said, "Thank you, sir, so very much for taking the time to see my Carlos. You are a very nice man."

Carlos was joining us at Harvard.

"I am so proud of you boys," Marisol said when the three of us got accepted, "but since Carlos has to take these extra courses this summer, I can't take you on a special graduation trip as I had planned."

That was news to us.

"So. You have to promise me that no matter what, after you finish your first year at college, we will all go for a trip that summer. Do you promise? No matter what? Jobs. Girlfriends. Nothing. Nothing gets in the way."

That's how the four of us went to Rome for six weeks in June and July of the summer after our freshman year in college.

We started in a rush and did all the must-see things. But then, after three weeks of non-stop walking and gawking and listening—we decided to devote out lives to languishing.

One night—while we were sipping grappa at the Spanish Steps—Carlos asked Marisol if she wanted to go to Barcelona.

"Why would I want to do that?" she asked.

"To go back home? To show it to us?"

Marisol took a sip of her grappa. She put the glass down on the little table and looked up at the black night sky.

"I will never return to Barcelona."

When Marisol gazed up at a night sky and made a pronouncement of elegant simplicity, it would be sacrilegious to say anything—never mind ask a question.

The moment was interrupted by a bride and groom and all their entourage descending the steps and posing for moonlit photographs.

"Look how she smiles," Marisol said. "Those are the smiles of the unknowing."

There wasn't much to do after that except return home.

The next thing we knew, we all graduated from Harvard and we all went to grad school. I was at Harvard Medical School and both Todd and Carlos were at MIT.

In med school, I developed two abiding interests: eye surgery and emergency medicine. They occurred simultaneously, when I did my

ER rounds. I could have specialized in eye surgery. But—the lure of the ER had me in its thrall.

I did my hospital match and got the assignment I wanted—the emergency department at Boston Health Clinic.

My friends, my teachers, my colleagues—everyone thought I should go to one of the very prestigious hospitals that courted me. Johns-Hopkins. Duke. Mount Sinai. New York Presbyterian.

"Forget the people who say you've made a mistake," Marisol said to me. "I know why you are doing this thing that everyone thinks is loco but it's a good thing to do."

"Why do you think I'm doing it?"

"Because of your mother and father."

I was taken aback and she knew it.

"There's nothing wrong with trying to help the world get better because you lost your mother and father," she said.

"Thank you, Mom."

That's how I ended up at BHC.

Carlos, in the meantime, got a super job working for NASA. The Jupiter Project. He was more-or-less based at MIT, but he would be in Houston a lot and also spend time at Cape Canaveral.

Todd did what we knew Todd would do. He discovered a new high-tech company that developed things that no one knew could be developed. The company was in Palo Alto and was called Livermore Solutions Unlimited. They hired him in a flash. He got a great salary and a signing bonus and a huge office and all the equipment and resources he needed. No one, neither Todd nor his boss, had any idea what he was supposed to do. He was just to do *something*.

There we were, then. Kind of like adults. Jobs. Income. Health insurance. 401(k)'s. Beneficiaries. Apartments. Cars. Work clothes.

The only problem with being an adult was that I couldn't go back.

It's like once you learn to walk, you can't go back to crawling.

After what happened next, I would have given anything to go back to the cradle and start over.

CHAPTER NINE
Consequences

Linda should have been different. That didn't come out exactly right. Well, no, actually, it was right. Linda should have been different. She should have been a different kind of person. But, of course, no one can be a different kind of person. We are who we all are.

I don't really know much about religion—next to nothing, if the truth be known. The God's honest truth—irony and all. But I think my views toward people make me a neo-Calvinist. We are pre-destined. That's all there is to it.

But we're not destined by fate. I don't believe in fate. I don't believe in things being pre-ordained. We are not at the whim of our births or of our stars.

We are at the whim of our actions.

Our actions are determined by who we are. That's what we can't change. We can't change who we are. So, by extension, we can't change what we do.

Carlos met Linda Bellanotte—a nice Italian girl, as Marisol would say—when he was still at Stanton Academy. Stanton, of course, is all boys. But Linda came to a track meet to watch her brother run the one-thousand meters.

Guillermo Bellanotte—a mouthful if I say so myself—was our classmate and Linda's brother. What a difference a name can make.

Tim Shaw. Guillermo Bellanotte.

Introduce me, and people think CPA.

Introduce him, and people think adventurer.

Guillermo won the thousand meters for us that day. After the race, he introduced his sister to Todd and me—and then, like an afterthought, to Carlos.

It was an afterthought because Guillermo was the same age as Todd and I—we were seniors—and his sister was eleven months younger. He only bothered to introduce Linda to Carlos because Carlos was standing there, sort of shuffling back and forth on his feet, nervously awaiting the fifty-five-meter hurdles race that he was about to run.

"Hi," he said to Linda. "Gotta run."

Which was literally the situation.

Todd and I fell over each other trying to one-up ourselves in Linda's eyes. But those eyes were darting away from us every few seconds. Linda had something on her mind. And it wasn't Double-D or me.

Carlos, the fool, never followed up with Linda. Not right away. He let a month go by and then he got up the nerve to call her and ask her to go to the Spring Fling.

The Fling is an annual weekend event at Stanton, that includes opening day for our baseball team, opening night for the drama club's annual original musical, the Fling into Spring Picnic on the Green, and the very formal Fling Dance.

Apparently, Linda said something like, "You waited a month to call?"

"I didn't have anything to ask you to," Carlos answered.

"What about a movie?"

"Oh."

"What about dinner?"

"Oh."

"What about—"

"Listen. Do you want to come to the Fling with me or not? You can stay here the whole weekend. The boys move out of the dorm and sleep on the gym floor in sleeping bags and the girls get to stay in the rooms. I didn't think of a movie or anything else because I didn't think of them. That's all there is to it."

"And you're an honors student?"

"Yes, I am."

"I'll cut you some slack."

"What does that mean?"

"It means I'm in. Do I need a formal dress?"

I hadn't thought anything could be worse than living with Carlos' mother and having her be unattainable—until I had to stand alone at the dance and watch Carlos move slowly across the floor with Linda. It was worse because, unlike Marisol, Linda *was* attainable. Here I was, standing like a fool in my rented tux—my first time in a tux—wondering why I didn't have a date—wondering if Linda might realize that Carlos wasn't for her and come running across the dance floor to me.

This—I said to myself—is pathetic. That was it for me. That was the turning point. There was a great wide world out there—full of wonderful girls—and I was going to stop moping and stop feeling sorry for myself and get into the game.

At that precise moment—like in a movie—a really great-looking girl ran up to me. She was crying.

I offered her my handkerchief and she wiped her eyes.

"Are you okay?" I asked.

"Do you know Steve Sullivan?"

"Yeah. He's a jerk."

"Dance with me."

Wow.

Life could work.

Her name was Missy Malone. That sounds like a stage name, but it was in fact her actual name. I danced with her. I got her a glass of punch. I sat with her on a leather settee in the corner of the room and we ate sugar cookies and then I put my hand on her shoulder and then the next thing I knew I was kissing her and the next thing I knew after that was that she was kissing me back.

It was a great night. Well, for me and Carlos. Todd actually had a date but she was the kind of girl who only wanted to see what other boys were there that she might date in the future. She was using Todd as an entry ticket to what she perceived as the choice crop of young men that Stanton Academy offered up to an unsuspecting world.

But Double-D could fend for himself.

And so could Carlos.

I was head over heels and didn't care one bit about what might happen. The only thing I knew was that this girl was kissing me and I wanted to do nothing else in this or any other world but to kiss her back.

This wasn't going where you may have thought it was going.

I wish it had.

Consequences be damned.

I wanted unwanted consequences.

I wanted unexpected consequences.

I wanted unsavory consequences.

I wasn't thinking about any of that really. All I was thinking about was how in the world would I unbutton her dress.

"Hey!"

The person shouting, "Hey!" was, of course, Steven Sullivan— eliciting the exact effect Missy was hoping for.

Within a minute, it was all over.

I was brushed aside.

Missy and Steven simultaneously accused each other of betrayal and simultaneously forgave each other and simultaneously were in each other's arms.

What could I do?

I walked outside and crossed the Green and went out to Brookline Avenue and got a cab and went home to tell Marisol the whole story.

"Tim," she said, "if that's the worst thing that ever happens to you because of love then consider yourself lucky."

Then she made us nachos supreme and we watched *Love Actually* on Netflix.

CHAPTER TEN
Ruin

Hold onto your hats because this happens awfully fast.

Linda was pregnant.

We were all out of grad school—we were in our new adult phase. Our careers were in full swing. Life held what appeared to be limitless promise.

I was a senior fellow at Boston Health Clinic. The ER was my domain and I loved it.

Todd had his plum job at Livermore—sitting in his technology-laden office, trying to decide what to work on that could possibly justify his enormous salary.

Carlos was analyzing data about Jupiter with the idea of sending a manned mission to that giant planet. They couldn't land on Jupiter, of course, as it's made of gas. But they could fly close to it and analyze it and send down a probe that would bring back samples. The cost for such a trip was something like eleven mazillion dollars—so the odds were it would never get off the drawing board; but the space guys and gals had fun planning it anyway.

Then there was Linda. Linda was a triple threat. She was a sports reporter for WLXV Channel 8 in Boston. She was a weekend on-air personality for the Golf Network. And—this was brand new—she was pretty close to announcing her candidacy for the U.S. House of Representatives.

"Linda is pregnant," Carlos said to me as he, Linda and I sat at a corner table in Starbucks on a gray and cold November morning.

"Congrat—" I started to say and then stopped dead.

The look on Linda's face stopped me.

"This," I said, "is not a welcome event?"

"I can't have a baby now," Linda said. "I can't stop for a baby now. How can I? How can I run for Congress—pregnant?"

"I don't know," I said. "I mean it's none of my business, of course, but wouldn't a baby be a positive thing for voters?"

"No. Maybe for some. But, no. And I'm not married. Most women will see me as irresponsible. Most men will see me as loose."

"In this day and age?"

She looked at me for a moment.

"Almost nothing has changed," she said. "Women are still judged by rules that are different from men's rules."

This went back and forth for fifteen minutes.

"And it is your business," Carlos said. "You're our friend. Our best friend. You and Todd. You're our best friends."

"I can't have a baby. Not now. I've thought this over every single moment of the day and night for a month. I've dreamed about this every night for a month. Even if I weren't going to run for the House, it would be a terrible time to have a baby. My sports career is on the verge of a new level. ESPN has approached me to announce Friday Night Baseball games. Not to be the woman down in the box seats talking to fans and mascots. Not to be the woman next to the announcer in the booth filling in as the color analyst. They want me to be the announcer. How could I have a baby with that looming? And then throw in a run for public office? No. It's not possible. No. I can't do it. I have to have an abortion."

"That is your choice, of course. What would you like me to do? I can certainly arrange it here. Keep it very discreet. I know Dr. Wilson in OB/GYN. There's no one better."

"No," Carlos said.

"No," Linda said.

"Oh. Would you prefer a woman doctor? Dr. Sara Jones is excellent. I could—"

"No," Linda said. "You're not getting it."

"Getting it? Getting what?" I asked.

"We want you to do it," Carlos said.

"What? No. Why would you want that? Obviously, I can do it. But you'd want someone with all the experience of either Dr. Wilson or Dr. Jones. It's commonplace for them. Their teams are all in place. Completely expert care."

"You," Linda said. "You alone. No teams. No one but you."

I looked at them both for a moment.

"You know I can't do that," I said.

"I know you can," Linda said.

"I cannot do that. That's not ethical. If we were on a desert island somewhere and it was an emergency, that would be a different story.

But we are here. In Boston. You have competent, safe, ethical care at your disposal. No. I couldn't do it. And— And— There's no need to worry about any word getting out."

"Of course there's the need to worry. That's exactly what I'm worried about!"

"Linda—"

"No," she screamed at me. "No. Never. I'm not going to throw away my career because some nurse or some orderly sees me and goes to the papers or TV."

"Or Tweets it. Or puts it on Instagram," Carlos added.

"Or even some husband or some boyfriend of a woman who's a patient. Can you guarantee me that I could come in, register, wait in the waiting room, go into pre-op, meet with nurses and the anesthesiologist, then go into the operating room, then go into recovery, then get dressed and check out and go outside and get into our car and drive home—without one single solitary human being seeing me? Can you guarantee that not one single person will see me?"

"Of course I couldn't guarantee that."

"That's why we said to meet us here," Carlos said. "We couldn't come to your office. We didn't want to meet with you on hospital grounds."

"Where?" I asked, "would you expect me to perform this procedure?"

"In my condo," Linda said.

"You're crazy," I said. "You're both crazy. You know how much I care about the two of you, but this is unethical and illegal. I cannot and I will not do this."

Of course I did it.

Because if I hadn't done it, there would be no story to tell. Not a story anyone would care about hearing.

But first, I bought a book. It was called, *Babies Are So Wonderful*. I gave it to Linda, with the hope that she would reconsider. Not because I thought she was wrong to have an abortion. I wanted her to reconsider because I thought it was wrong that I do it for her.

She took the book and flipped through it for a couple of seconds and then threw it down on the floor.

"Is that what you do with all your patients?" she asked.

"No. Only the ones who want me to do something I know I shouldn't do."

"If you won't help me—I will find someone who will."

That was that.

I did it—because I knew I could do it. I knew they would go to someone else if I refused. Possibly some hack.

I knew I could do it safely and efficiently. All by myself. In her condo. I had no doubt that I could do it. I had no doubt that there would be no complications. I had no doubt that Linda would be fine. I had no doubt there would be no future ramifications. She and Carlos could have a hundred kids later on if they wanted to.

Of course they didn't have a hundred kids later on.

They didn't have any kids later on.

They never married.

They were never together.

Linda committed suicide three days after the procedure.

The procedure—as I knew it would—went very smoothly. Linda was fine. I watched her very carefully after we were done—to make sure she was okay and there wasn't excessive bleeding or a drop in blood pressure or anything that might indicate a problem.

Linda was up and about within an hour. She had some tea and some dry toast. We talked about her future. She was going to declare her candidacy for the House in two weeks. As a Democrat running in Massachusetts, she had a near lock on the election. It was hers to lose. She knew she was safe, because no one could possibly leak the story of her abortion to the press. The only people who knew were Carlos and me. She was safe. She had come through wonderfully. She had nothing but promise ahead of her.

Carlos came by at night, and I stayed with them until midnight.

I returned at 7:00 A.M. and found her in perfect health and in great spirits. She was quite thankful. She was ebullient. Her career was safe. He future was secure.

I left at 9:00 A.M. and went straight to work at the hospital.

Linda went about her life as usual for the next couple of days. She and Carlos talked it all out and seemed at ease with themselves.

But then, three days after the abortion, at about 9:45 A.M, as best as we could figure out, Linda sat at her kitchen table and wrote a note.

Dear Carlos,

I've done a terrible thing. I've taken a life. It's not your fault. It's not Tim's fault. I insisted he perform the abortion. I insisted on everything. It was my decision. My decision alone. And there's nothing I can do to undo what I've done. I can't live with myself. There is no other option. I've never loved anyone but you, Carlos. Ever since I saw you run the hurdles in high school. I fell in love with you that day and I've been in love with you every day since. I'm so sorry.

~Linda

Carlos called me from her condo. He had gotten there at 10:00 A.M.—in time to find ambulances and fire trucks and police cars everywhere.

He had gotten there in time to see a blanket-covered body laying on the sidewalk, five stories below the open window of Linda's condo.

Carlos, sobbing uncontrollably, told me what happened.

I kept thinking this can't be true. Was she dead? Maybe she was injured but still alive? Maybe it was someone else? Maybe—?

I realized after a while that Carlos had gone silent on the phone.

"Carlos— Are you there?"

He was there.

"I'm inside her condo," he said. "I came up here to see— To see— To see the window."

"I'm on my way," I said.

"There's no time."

"What do you mean, Carlos?"

"The police will be up here soon."

"Yes?"

"What do you think I should do with this note?"

"What note? Did you find a note?"

"I found a note," he said. "It was folded in half—and it was sticking out of the book. The book you gave her about babies."

I didn't say a word.

He read it to me.

He didn't sob.

He didn't falter.

He read the note to me—as if Linda were talking to me.

"What should I do with this note?" he demanded. "What do you think I should do with this note that I found in the book about babies that you had given to Linda? Huh? Tim? What should I do with this note?"

"Give it to the police," I said. "Let what happens happen, Carlos. I'm not going to deny her family. They have the right to know what happened. And—I'm not going to deny justice. Let what happens happen, Carlos. Show the police the note. I'm on my way."

He hung up.

I lost my license. I was banned from practicing medicine forever. You should have seen them swarm. The jackals. I never denied it. I never tried to explain it. I didn't ask for mercy. I didn't ask for a break. I told them everything that happened.

"I did what I did because she was my friend and she was desperate and I wanted to help her. The procedure was done accurately and safely. I stayed with her and then went back the next day and the day after that and there was nothing—nothing—to suggest she was troubled. I did it because I was afraid she would go to someone else where she would be at great risk medically. I was wrong to do it. I should not have done it. But I did what I did to help my friend."

In exchange for my signature on a document admitting my mistake and agreeing never to practice medicine in the United States ever again, I was promised that I would not face criminal charges. There was no publicity. No one knew anything. Not even Todd or Marisol.

I was allowed to slink away.

Linda's father was an attorney with a lot of clout in City Hall—so the newspapers reported that Linda Bellanotte committed suicide for no known reason. The sports channels ran tributes to her career, and the Democratic party issued a statement that the state had lost a woman who would have been a great public servant.

On the same day, three terrorists were arrested at Logan Airport trying to bring handguns on a flight to Paris and that pushed all other news to the side for a week.

Linda Bellanotte was allowed to be buried in peace.

Carlos was not implicated at all. I lied to everyone and said that all conversations were between Linda and me alone. There was nothing to be gained by dragging Carlos into it.

But Carlos was dragged into it. By himself. He was trapped in his isolation. The only person he could talk to about it was me—and there was nothing left to say to me.

So Carlos returned to work and sat in his office and looked at maps of Jupiter and did nothing. Within a month he was fired. He didn't care. He welcomed it. Why should he work on man taking flight to glory? When Linda took flight from her window, all glory was left behind.

Then it actually got worse.

If what had happened had been a cake, then this would have been the icing.

Two months after Linda's death, Carlos and Marisol were at my apartment for dinner—when Todd suddenly appeared. Out of the blue.

Of course, he had come home for the funeral and to help Carlos and me and Marisol.

Then he had returned to California to work.

But here he was. Strangely. For no apparent reason.

Dropped off by a cab from the airport. He hadn't even called to be picked up.

He sat at the dining-room table. I poured him a glass of pinot noir.

He took a sip. Looked at us. Smiled.

"Why are you here?" I asked him.

"Nothing there anymore."

"What do you mean? What happened?"

"Bust. Livermore Solutions Unlimited went bust. Every penny lost. Not one penny left."

"That's terrible," I said.

"Every penny I had as well."

"What?"

"They gave me a chance to buy in as a partner. I gave them everything I had. I got a great office."

Todd laughed and his laughter broke the seal.

"Well," I said, "Guess what?"

"What?"

"There's nothing left for any of us?"

"Huh?"

"That man Shel is a pig," Marisol said. "A greedy filthy pig."

What we now had to tell Todd was that none of us had any money. Shel Crummins had taken all of us for a ride.

"What in the world happened?" Todd asked.

"It's that pig, Shel Crummins. Crummy Pig. That's what I call him. Crummy Pig."

"What happened to the money?"

"The Crummy Pig took it."

"Mom," I said, "let me explain."

"What is there to explain, Timothy? We had money. Then Crummy Pig took our money. Now we have no money. What else is there to— explain?"

"Shel put our money into land annuities," I said to Double-D by way of explanation.

"Wait. Whose money?"

"All of us. Me, you, Carlos and Mom."

"I heard Timothy talking to Carlos about the money," Marisol said. "And I said I wanted to invest my money too. I gave him all of my money. All the money I had."

"All of my money is gone?" Todd asked. "My half of the money we got from selling the two houses?"

"Your half. My half. And then everything Carlos and Mom had as well."

"But," Todd said, "when did I agree to that?"

"We both agreed to that, apparently, when we signed all those papers way back when we first met Shel—"

"Don't call him that," Marisol snapped. "Call him Crummy Pig."

"At any rate," I continued, "when we first met with—Crummy Pig—we signed all kinds of papers giving him and the bank authority to invest our money any way they thought. Apparently, he did the same thing with Mom."

"So?" Todd asked.

"So?" I answered.

"So what happened to the money?"

"Crummy Pig stole it."

I put my hand up to hold Marisol back and then told Todd that our money had been invested in a land company called AngleShoals.

"I hate this AngleShoals as much as I hate Crummy Pig," Marisol shouted.

Todd kept asking questions and I kept holding Marisol at bay trying to answer.

"Basically, he told us—after the fact—that we should have doubled our money in three years. Except that all of that money was rolled over into AngleShoals. So he put every penny we had into the same fund."

"Crummy Pig said that this was a special investment," Marisol fumed. "That this company, this AngleShoals, was going to be sold and it was going to go way up in value. It was going to be a private transaction. Not in the store."

"The market," I corrected. "Not in the stock market."

"That's what Crummy Pig told us. So there was no omission."

"No commission," I said.

"Yes," Marisol said. "Yes. That's right, Timothy. Thank you, Timothy, for always being so happy to correct my English."

I sort of nodded my head to indicate I was sorry.

"Anyway," Marisol continued, "Crummy Pig took a fee. A fee for finding this investment. He called it a finder's fee. Isn't that right, Timothy?"

"Yes, Mom. Sorry, Mom."

"I think this is our fault," Marisol said. "For wanting to make so much money. We let Crummy Pig handle everything because we were greedy. And we were punished! Punished! Punished for being greedy!"

"But—?" Todd asked, "how did all this transpire? What was the sequence of events?"

"Oh," I said. "Well, we knew nothing about this at all. Then we got a statement from Boston United Savings Bank that all of our money had been used to buy shares of AngleShoals—minus a finder's fee of three-million dollars."

"What?" Todd yelled. "Three million dollars? And you went along with that?"

"There was nothing to be done," I said. "It had happened. We demanded a meeting."

"Oh, a meeting was a good idea," Todd said, sarcastically.

"Look," I said. "now—looking at it now—of course it was stupid on our part. We all simply signed everything away. You included, Todd. But—then—when we did it—what did we know about finance? We had lost Mom and Dad. Uncle Elliot took most of what we had. We met with Crummins. He said he would take care of us. It seemed reasonable. It seemed like a reasonable thing to do."

"Like operating on my girlfriend in her apartment," Carlos said. "Did that seem like the reasonable thing to do?"

"Carlos—"

"Don't even try to talk to me about Linda. You killed Linda."

"Carlos, I didn't—"

"Carlos!"

It was Marisol shouting at her son.

"Carlos, what in the world are you talking about?"

"He killed Linda. That's what I'm talking about."

So it had to come out.

More icing on an already over-iced cake.

Marisol and Todd had both thought—because of what I told them—that I was out of medicine for writing an incorrect prescription that inadvertently resulted in a patient's death. They both thought that my absence was temporary. For one year. They had no idea that I was linked to Linda's suicide.

"You mean—you cannot be a doctor again?" Marisol asked.

"No. Never. I can never practice medicine again."

"Which is what he deserved," Carlos said.

"It was her idea!" I yelled. "It was your idea! You begged me to do it."

Carlos stared hard at me.

"You gave her that book," he said.

For the first time in the years I had known him, I saw something inside Carlos that was not kind.

"You gave her that book," he said again. "I found the note in that book that you gave her. That book killed her."

"She threatened to do it without me. Where? In some back alley? You threatened to risk her life if I didn't help. I didn't want to do it. It wasn't right for me to do it. I gave her that book because it was the only way I could think of to try and get her to change her mind. You should have told her not to do it. You sided with her. She loved you. If anyone killed her, it was you—not me."

"You bastard!"

Carlos jumped at me and pushed me hard and I went flying into the wall. Then he was on top of me and striking me with his fists.

I fought back. I had to fight back. It took me a moment to get over the shock but then I started lashing out at him. We rolled over and over on the floor, each of us pummeling the other for all we were worth.

Marisol was screaming at us to stop.

"Todd! Stop them!"

But Todd didn't move.

Marisol screamed at him again—but Todd didn't move.

Marisol ran to us, but Todd put his hands on Marisol to restrain her.

"Let them work it out."

"They will kill each other."

"No they won't."

We didn't kill each other.

There was blood. But—not enough to die over.

We were on our way up, trying to stand, and Carlos swung at me and his fist hit me on the side of my head. The pain was like an electric volt of fury.

My God, I thought, that feels good.

I swung at him, but I missed and that hurt almost as much. My arm wrenched itself. I shook it off and turned to the side to absorb another shot from Carlos and then both of us fell to the floor again.

He pushed. I pushed.

We rolled away from each other.

We were burnt out. We lay on the floor breathing hard and staring at each other.

"I loved her so much," Carlos cried.

"I know. I know."

"I miss her so much."

"I know."

"It—it wasn't your fault, Tim."

"It wasn't anyone's fault," I said.

We were on our knees—facing each other.

"We ruined our lives," Carlos said. "We lost Linda. You lost who you are. I lost who I am."

"We'll never get Linda back," I said. "Maybe—maybe we can get ourselves back."

"Not if it costs more than twenty bucks," Todd said.

Good for Double-D.

We needed that.

Carlos and I couldn't help but laugh at that.

"There is nothing funny about Crummy Pig," Marisol said.

She almost laughed. She almost cried.

"This is more than I can bear," she said. "Poor Linda. Poor Tim. Poor Carlos. I don't know if I can even think about this. It is more than I can bear."

She looked at us on the floor.

She spoke to us as she had spoken to us that night at the foot of the Spanish Steps.

"No it isn't," she said. "No it isn't. I can bear this. I can take this. We can all take this. Nothing can ruin us. I will take care of it. I swear to you that I will find a way to take care of it. Get up, my boys. Get up off of the floor and let me take care of you."

"We're okay," I said, straining a bit to get up.

I reached down and offered Carlos a hand.

He looked at it. Then he clasped it with his hand and I pulled him up.

We looked at each other and smiled.

"I haven't been in a fistfight since—since I don't know when," I said.

"It wasn't a very good fight," Carlos said.

"Good enough," I replied.

"Yeah," Carlos said, "good enough."

There should have been a pause at this point and then someone should have said something profound about friendship. About loss. About grief. About finding a way to push ahead.

But Todd had money on his mind.

"All the money is gone?" Todd asked.

We all laughed again.

"All the money is gone," I said.

We took our seats at the table and nursed our wounds—such as they were—and poured more wine and passed around a plate of Marisol's homemade sticky buns that she had brought with her.

"So?" Todd asked, "what happened—at your—meeting?"

"Well, the first meeting was at the beginning—about the huge finder's fee."

"Why didn't you call me?" Todd asked.

"It was two days ago. This all just happened. The first meeting was just two days ago."

"A meeting with all the Crummy Pigs," Marisol said

"All? Who's all?"

"The bank president—Jonathan Slocum," I said. "And two vice presidents—Clive Williams and Mario Mollacare. They had all kinds of paperwork to show that the fee was fair and equitable. They convinced us that we had nothing to worry about. The money would be working for us. Silently. AngleShoals did not release earnings statements in order to avoid the competition getting an advantage. But they—the four of them—assured us that they personally guaranteed that all of our money was safe and was going to grow exponentially."

"So we thanked them very much and we went home," Marisol said.

"I was going to call you, but it was late and I thought that everything was under control—sort of. I didn't know what to think about the finder's fee—but I thought that the rest of our money, our investment, was safe."

"And then—?" Todd asked.

"This morning, I got an email from an attorney in Miami that was so poorly written that I thought it was a joke. One of those letters from the Prince of Nigeria sort of thing. I had my finger on the delete button when I re-read the last sentence that said that even though our entire investment was gone, they might be able to sue on our behalf and re-coup perhaps 10 percent of it. Of which they would take a third."

"Tim called Crummy Pig," Marisol said, "and Crummy Pig said that we had nothing left and if he could ever help us in the future please give him a phone call."

"What?"

"It was true," I said. "What the Miami lawyer wrote was true. There was nothing left. AngleShoals had gone bankrupt. They came out with their annual statement and reported that there was no money left. Not a penny. Our money was gone. We checked, of course. And it was gone. Lots of people lost money. They really did go bankrupt. That's why Carlos and Mom came here tonight to eat dinner. To talk about this. And then you show up and you have bad—"

"But—" Todd stammered.

No buts about it. Our money was gone.

"We were going to call you in a while," I said. "Since we thought you were in California and you would still be at work until just about now. We were going to call you and let you know what happened to-day."

"Well, here I am. So, what happened today?" Todd asked.

We went there," I said. "We stormed in and demanded to see Crummins and the others. They smirked at us. They pretended to be, oh, so concerned, but they were smirking. They said that the bank was not liable. They said that this sort of thing happens. It's a risk. A risk we knew we were getting into and that we signed off on."

"But," Carlos threw in, "Mollacare wasn't at the meeting."

"That's right," I said. "Crummins was there and Williams and Slocum were there. But Mollacare wasn't there."

"Because," Carlos added, "he had been—reassigned—they said—to be a branch manager. That's a huge demotion, of course, but they said it was a change in direction. Don't you love that double speak? They said the change in direction had nothing to do with our investment, but I know they were lying."

"So we left," Carlos said.

"We went to Dad's lawyers," I said to Todd. "Right after the bank, we drove to Dad's lawyers' office and they sat with us and we showed them all the paperwork and they told us that there was nothing to be done. Nothing could be done. We could try suing the bank—but there was no evidence that they knew the deal was doomed."

"Of course they knew!" Carlos shouted.

"All the Crummy Pigs knew!" Marisol shouted as well.

"I know," I said. "I didn't want to believe it. But— I know. I know Crummins knew. I know AngleShoals gave Crummins such an exorbitant finder's fee to make him invest before they went bankrupt. Crummins handed them our money. And they did God-knows-what with it. Probably in some Byzantine offshore account."

"There's no recourse?" Todd asked.

"Our lawyers said no. Because the bank did indeed warn us in writing about the risk. No one ever reads those things, of course. You just sign them. But—on paper—the bank was on solid ground. The best offer we had was from the illiterate Miami lawyer, but then—this evening—we got another email from his office saying that he had been indicted for jury tampering—a charge he of course denies—and he was devoting his time to proving his innocence and would take no new cases. Besides, Dad's lawyers said that would have gotten us nowhere except to lose more money in what they call incidental fees."

"All of it is gone," Marisol said. "Every little penny."

"Money," Carlos said. "Linda. Tim's career. My career. Todd's career."

"That's a hell of a lot of bad stuff," Todd said. "You've got to admire a fate that could deal such a hand in such a brief time."

"I don't admire none of them," Marisol said. "None of the Crummy Pigs. But—believe me, my boys, we will make this okay. I am so sad about Linda and what that tragedy has done to you, Timothy, and to you, my Carlos. And I am so sad for you, Todd. My Double-D. To me, Double-D—it stands for Dear Darling."

Todd broke into a wide smile.

He put his hand across the table and Marisol reached out and put her hand on top of his. Carlos and I did likewise.

"Listen to me, my boys," Marisol said. "We will be okay. We have no money. But we have our brains. We have faith in each other. We have this house. Most of all—I say this to the sky above—we have me."

CHAPTER ELEVEN
Out of Our Hands

That's how we all came to live with Mom again.

Carlos, Todd and I moved in to the big house on Beacon Hill. We weren't paupers yet. We had enough money to get by on. We could pay all our bills each month. We could go out to eat and see movies and buy clothes. We just couldn't do it forever. In actuality, we could only do it for five months. Then we'd be broke. *Then* we'd be paupers. Marisol would lose the house and we'd be out on the street. We'd have really nice clothes to wear out on the street. But we'd be out there nonetheless.

"Well, we need jobs," I said. "That's pretty obvious."

"I could teach school," Marisol said.

We looked at her.

"Mom?" Carlos asked.

"What, my Carlos?"

"What do you mean you could teach school?"

"I could teach school. Not college. But I could teach high school. I saw your work at Stanton. I met the teachers. I could do that."

"Well—" Todd said. "I'm sure you could do it. If you set your mind to it. But—you know—you have to have a college degree. And it helps if you have a master's degree. And you need to be certified if you're going to teach in public schools."

"And—" I reluctantly added, "it would help if you had teaching experience. Even a little."

Marisol shut her eyes for a moment. Then she opened them and said, "I could work in a restaurant."

"Mom. I don't want my mother to work as a waitress."

"Waitress?" she said. "Waitress? I would be the woman out front who greets the customers as they come in."

"The hostess," I said. "Oh, you'd be great at that."

"Thank you."

"But we don't want you to work," I hastily added. "We'll get jobs and take care of bills and the house. It's all our fault that you're in this mess. And we'll take care of it."

Todd took control and laid out a plan. Each of us would look for a job, right away. Starting the next morning. Todd—in mathematics. Carlos—in engineering. Me—in medicine.

None of us, not even Todd, thought that this was a good plan.

"Of course," Todd said, "I think that after my company failed so spectacularly, other companies would be—uncertain—about bringing me aboard."

"I'm not working anywhere," Carlos said. "I can't. I can barely sit here now and talk to you guys. I'm only doing it for Mom."

"And I can't work in medicine. I'll never work as a doctor again. I have been approached by three pharma companies. To sell drugs for them. No salary. No benefits. Commission only. I'd have to go back and try and sell new drugs to doctors I know who I've worked with."

"We will not let you do that," Marisol said, raising her voice.

"Thank you," I said. "You don't have to be concerned. I told them all to go to hell."

"Good for you," Marisol said. "Hell is what those *bastardos* deserve. May they burn in hell for all of the years to come."

Once Marisol got going about hell fire and those who deserve it, there was no stopping her for at least a half hour. We sat back and listened to her call for fiery retribution on Shel Crummins and on Boston United Savings Bank and on all its employees and on all the money in its vaults and on all of the pens on little chains that never have ink and on all of the little calendars on the counters that never have the right date.

"Why can they not have ink? The bank has tons and tons of money. And they can't buy ink for those little pens? I hate them and their little pens."

Of course, Marisol was forced to grant one dispensation from her fireball—for me.

Because, as it would turn out, a little over three weeks later I went to work for Boston United Savings Bank.

CHAPTER TWELVE
Mr. Clean

I went to work for the bank—in a circuitous way—because I bumped into Steven Sullivan while walking to the Green Line stop near the Boston Public Library.

Do you remember Steven? He was the guy Missy Malone wanted to spite at the Fling Dance at Stanton. She made out with me, hoping he'd notice, which he did. They left the dance and me in the dust.

Ah, getting dumped for the first time. You never forget it.

"Tim? Tim Shaw?"

"Steve? Steve Sullivan? My God. How the hell are you?"

With the obligatory chit-chat, we learned that Steven and Missy had indeed married.

"Then, after two years, she left me for my younger brother," Steven said.

"That must make Christmas a lot of fun," I ventured.

Steven laughed.

"Good riddance to both of them. I haven't seen either one in three years and I hope to never see either one again."

He was amazed at what happened to me.

Then I told him about Todd and Carlos and Marisol.

"Wow."

"Yeah," I said, " wow."

"You know what I mean. Bummer."

"Yeah," I said. "Bummer."

"So, what are you doing for money?"

"Well, I need a job. That's why I was here at the library. I was at a speed-networking event. You know. Like dating. Except there are employers sitting at a long row of tables and they ring a bell every three minutes and all the potential employees move over one spot."

"You get a job?"

"No. Nothing there for me."

He looked at me.

"There's nothing anywhere for me," I said. "I'm nearing the end of my rope."

"Then it's a good thing we bumped into each other," Steven said. "Not to mention—I owe you one."

Steven was an entrepreneur of sorts. He owned some apartment buildings in Chelsea. He was part owner in a car service that catered to doctors at Boston hospitals. He bought a bankrupt rug-cleaning business—Casper Carpets.

"You want me to clean carpets?" I asked.

"No. No. Not at all. I don't go anywhere near Casper Carpets. I have a manager who runs the whole thing. I don't really care about it. I got it for a song. The owner was an alcoholic gambler who lost everything he had betting on the Patriots in Superbowl XLII. And then he tried to make it all back in Superbowl XLVI. Anyway. He lost every-thing. Got divorced. His kids disowned him. I've heard they became Giants fans. Anyway, I bought his company so cheaply—all he wanted was money for a bus ticket to Canada. Well, a little more than that. So, I don't care what happens to the business."

"Why are you telling me this?"

"Oh. Well, I went to an industrial-cleaning-services trade show in Toronto. Trade shows are great for making contacts. You go to a trade show, you can forget your speed-dating nonsense. So. I met this guy who cleans buildings. He was looking for a partner and I now own 40 percent of his business."

"Are you saying there's a job for me there?"

"What? No. Not at all. But—here's the part that may interest you. My new partner—Bill Planter—he knows a guy that is looking to sell his business. This guy—his name is— Let me think— Begins with an 'S.' Slander. No, that can't be it. Slender. No. Slentil. That's it. Rhymes with 'lentil.' Oscar Slentil. That's it. Anyway, Oscar Slentil—I've never met him by the way—Oscar Slentil is a little like Casper. The rug guy. Slentil is in debt big time and probably will have to declare bankruptcy—but that wouldn't help him with back taxes. Or—and this is where someone smart comes in—he sells the whole thing for a lousy ten thousand dollars—which to Slentil is a whole lot of money these days—and the buyer would have to pay the back taxes. The taxes are something like two hundred thousand dollars. But—the odds are the IRS would work out a deal with the new owner. See? This could be what you're looking for."

"You want me to buy Slentil's company?"

"Of course. That's why I'm telling you."

"If this is such a good deal, why don't you and this Planter guy buy it?"

"I'm stretched out too far. And so is Planter. That's why he needed my money. He's barely keeping his head above water. But my money is going to fix everything and get us going again. And I plan on being very rich by this time next year. But right now, I can't afford any new deals."

"What— What does this Slentil guy do?"

"Oh. That would help, wouldn't it. He cleans banks. That's his job. He owns a company that cleans banks. He never expanded. It's his niche. He calls the company BankJob. Get it? Kind of funny."

"Unless, he robs the banks," I said.

"He can't. He'd be the first person they'd suspect. He's crooked enough to do it. But he's just barely smart enough to know they'd nail him within hours. It's always the cleaning company. That's what the cops think. It's always the cleaning company."

And that, boys and girls, is how I got to meet Oscar Slentil and buy his company for eight thousand dollars and a one-way plane ticket to Las Vegas.

I was going to change the company name, but, oddly enough, there was equity in that name. People knew it. Banks knew it. No point in starting from scratch if we didn't have to.

The "we" is of course Todd, Carlos and me.

"You're going to do what?" Marisol asked. "You're going to do what?"

"Clean banks."

"Clean banks?"

"I've bought a company that specializes in cleaning banks."

"What do you mean—clean banks?"

"It's a business, Mom. It's a business. They clean banks. You know. Vacuum the rugs. Throw out the trash. Clean the windows. Wipe down the counters. Iron the money."

"Iron—"

"I'm kidding. But all the other stuff is true. I bought a company. I used nearly every penny I had left. So I own a company.They have two trucks. Two vans. All kinds of equipment. Vacuums. Sprayers. Squeegees."

"Do they have employees?" Todd asked.

"No. Everyone quit when they didn't get paid."

"Do they have clients?"

"Yes and no. They had at one time thirty clients. Well, six banks, with five branches each. Thirty buildings. They lost all of them. However, it's not as bad as it seems. Because two of the clients—ready for this—New England Mutual of Boston and Boston United Savings Bank—Dad's bank and our bank—"

"What?" Marisol screamed. "You're not going to work for Crummy Pig, are you?"

"No. No. I don't even meet with the bank. With any bank. Turns out the banks have a clearinghouse that buys stuff that all the banks need. Like pens with no ink! So my deal is with the clearinghouse. I will have no contact with any of our Crummy Pigs. Anyway, the clearinghouse hasn't gotten a replacement yet for those two banks. If I move fast, and impress them and give them a discount rate—I may be able to get them back on board and that will be a start. From there we grow."

Marisol nodded and then raised one finger up—to make a point.

"And what about Todd and Carlos?"

I looked at both of them.

"Gentlemen, want to be partners? I don't need investment money—not right now at any rate. But I could use some sweat equity. First we need to clean out the office. Oh, I forgot. Slentil had rented an office in West Roxbury, on John Adams Street. It's really a garage with a back room. Anyway, I went there and the landlord, a guy named Fred Wills, was glad to meet me. He was stuck with everything and with three month's unpaid rent. So I agreed to settle the account and agreed to a one-year lease. Oh, I could use six thousand dollars for that. Three thousand from each of you? We'll split everything evenly of course. I'm getting ahead of myself. Listen. First, we have to clean it all up. The place. The office. The two vans. The equipment. Then we've got to start cleaning banks!"

"This is so crazy," Todd said. "We're Harvard grads, we were professionals, we were making tons of money. And now we're emptying trash and vacuuming rugs."

"Don't forget ironing the money," Marisol said.

Todd's point had no effect on me.

Sure, on the one hand, the three of us were throwing away all the education and expertise we had amassed through years of very hard work.

But I chose to look at it differently. We weren't throwing away anything. We were simply putting those things aside. It would be like you were a great basketball player and deciding one day not to pursue basketball anymore and instead become a history teacher. You wouldn't be wasting your basketball skill—you'd be developing a new skill.

The four of us discussed this over a really huge dinner that Marisol made, as I took notes in one of those black-and-white composition books. I've always liked those books. They are the essence of school.

"There's nothing to be gained by thinking about what we've lost," Carlos said. "Look at me. I've lost a father and a brother I never knew I had. And—I've lost Linda."

"We lost our mother and father," Todd said.

"And now," I put in, "we have this new family of ours and we have a new business. And as Mom would say"—I nodded to Marisol—'Nothing in this world is forever.' "

"That's right, Tim. I say that all the time. All the time I say, 'Nothing is forever.' "

Todd and Carlos agreed—this weird opportunity had come along, and we may as well give it a shot. If it failed, we wouldn't be out that much money; if it was successful, we could sell the business and use the money to do something we wanted to do.

None of us wanted to clean banks for a living.

We were going to clean banks to make a living.

"Nothing is forever," Marisol intoned, sliding out more tacos onto our plates from a huge frying pan. "See. I said it again."

CHAPTER THIRTEEN
Up and Running

I admit I got a rush when I stepped inside the garage on John Adams Street.

This is my company, I thought. I own this. This is something I can work on with my own hands. This is something I can build.

It dawned on me that that was probably what drove Dad to rebuild the Cessna. It's one thing to buy something; it's one thing to own something; it's quite another thing to build something.

We got to work.

The actual cleaning was easy. We took everything out of the garage and then swept out the whole area and threw away tons of stuff. We realized that some day we could discover that some of the things we were throwing away might be useful—but we couldn't look that far ahead. We needed the place to be clean. We needed everything to be in a neat pile or to be hung neatly on hooks on the walls. It was our mathematical bent.

The two vans were another matter. Both ran, but they made strange noises. Luckily, there was a service station across the street—it was run by a guy named Augie. I instantly liked Augie. We had a rapport and I trusted him implicitly.

As Augie worked on both vans, the three of us went into the office and tried to make sense of it. We applied the same modus operandi. We took everything out. We swept it clean. We only brought back things we thought we needed.

At the end of one very long day, the place was clean, the vans were purring and the files were organized.

The clearinghouse called and said we had a deal.

Which meant there was no excuse whatsoever for us not to clean a bank.

At 6:00 P.M. the next day, the three of us drove one of our vans up to the back entrance of the Boston United Savings Bank on Iron Street in South Boston. I used a key card and we were inside.

We stood in the middle of the bank.

"Where do we start?" Todd asked.

"I have no idea," I said. "I thought—I don't know—I thought it would be obvious what had to be done."

"Haven't you guys ever cleaned anything?" Carlos asked. "Did you ever clean your room?"

"Not if we could help it," I said.

"It's simple," Carlos said. "One of us empties all the trash and straightens out everything. All the chairs are put in place; all the pens are in the holders; all of those deposit slips and withdrawal slips are neatly arranged in their proper slots. Another one of us sprays every hard surface with that green liquid in those big bottles and wipes it all down. Meanwhile, the third guy is vacuuming."

I vacuumed.

Todd wiped the walls and counters and windows.

69

Carlos emptied trash and straightened out all the stuff.

We were done by 9:00.

"Well," Todd said as we were driving back to the office, "that was nearly enjoyable."

"Good hard work is never anything to be ashamed about," Carlos said.

"I can't wait to hire a crew," I said.

"Me too," Carlos said.

"Sooner the better," Todd said.

Five months went by. We were up to nineteen buildings. We got the cleaning time down to two hours.

Money was coming in.

The clearinghouse loved us.

We cleaned banks at night and worked in our office during the day.

Todd did all the bookkeeping. Carlos was in charge of the vans and supplies. I was responsible for getting new clients.

All in all, we'd be in the office for maybe four hours and then we'd be out cleaning for another six hours or so. It was a grind. We felt good about it. But it was a grind.

Then in quick succession I met the three Alonzos and I fell in love.

CHAPTER FOURTEEN
People

I didn't fall in love with one of the Alonzos. The falling in love part of this story comes a bit later.

But hiring the Alonzos freed up a lot of my time. Time I could devote to developing new business. And that's how I got to—well, let that wait its turn.

The bottom line is that you can't run a business without people. Preferably good people.

I was very happy when the Alonzos showed up at our office. Juanita Alonzo was the leader of their pack. She was the talker—both in terms of amount of words spoken and in grasp of the English language. Juanita could have been pretty if she had taken the bother. Her husband, Hermann, was the very silent type. A small wiry man, with a perpetual grizzled beard that always looked like it was about nine hours old. Then there was Luis, Hermann's brother. Luis was a giant. A huge man. Almost a scary man.

I hired the three of them on the spot and went out with them to our next assignment and showed them the ropes.

Not only were they all green-card legitimate workers, they worked harder than I could have imagined. They got the time for each job down to an hour. Once they did a bank in forty minutes.

Working from 6:00 P.M. To 3:00 A.M., and accounting for travel, they could do five banks a night. I had added more clients, but with the Alonzo Clan at my disposal, I could get all the jobs done, done right, and even do a bonus visit to each bank every two weeks.

Our clients were impressed.

Todd, Carlos and I took turns going out at night on jobs and supervising the Alonzos; and we spent the other days doing office work.

We had now been at it a year.

We paid all of our bills—rent and insurance, gas and oil and repairs for the trucks, cleaning supplies and cleaning equipment.

We were paying off the back taxes at a reasonable rate that we'd negotiated with the IRS.

We paid the Alonzos and gave them some basic benefits.

And we each took a modest salary of $45,000 a year.

We lived on that—including Marisol, of course—who we assuaged by putting her in charge of decorating our office. We gave her a budget of eighty dollars. She did a good job.

We were surviving. This was not what any of us had ever intended, this was not where any of us ever thought our careers would go. But it was honest work. We had a sense of accomplishment. We were all living in the same house with Marisol. We had great meals and great times doing simple things. We worked more-or-less regular hours. Or I should say we worked set hours. We were up late a lot, and we were up early a lot. But we weren't working 80 hours a week. We weren't working 60 hours a week. Life was going along smoothly and I think I can say that we were happy.

All right, maybe not happy.

Carlos still mourned the loss of Linda every day of his life. I still mourned the loss of Linda every day of my life.

Todd and I still mourned the loss of Mom and Dad.

Marisol still mourned the loss of little Martinez.

Nothing makes up for loss. Over the years, though, we took our hits, we took our misfortunes and we looked all of it in the face—and we moved forward. Not in a direction any of us every would have imagined. But it was forward. If you can move forward, if you can stay ahead of the game, then you can be content.

We wouldn't go so far as to say we were happy. But we would admit to being content.

CHAPTER FIFTEEN
Toronto

I didn't go to Toronto to fall in love. I went to Toronto to attend a trade show—to learn what was going on in the industry and to try and find ways to expand our business.

It was a two-day show and it turned out to be a waste of time. I left about a hundred business cards with people, but I knew nothing would ever come of it. I met tons of people walking along the booths, but there were no real prospects.

I had a flight leaving for Boston at 6:00 P.M., and it had been snowing since 3:00 P.M. I was in a taxi on the way to the airport when I got a text from the airline saying the flight had been canceled.

This was salt in the wound.

From the cab I called Avis and reserved a car and told my cabby to change our destination.

I got to the rental office—to find a long line of aggravated people waiting to get a car. I had a reservation—but it wasn't going to go smoothly, I could see that. The woman standing in front of me was grumbling about everything. She was a royal pain. I knew that instantly. She whined and complained and cursed everyone.

I admit that I smiled when she got up to the counter and was told there were no more cars. She blew up at the girl, to no avail, as if that would ever help.

She stormed away, promising to call down unholy demons to curse the company and all the employees—and she threw in all the cars for good measure.

I got my car, a red Mustang—which made me smile. I gathered up my papers and was walking toward the parking lot when I saw the angry woman standing in front of me. Waiting.

I tried to avoid eye contact and almost made it by her.

"Did I hear you're driving to Boston?"

I should have lied. I should have said Chicago.

But I instinctively tell the truth—that's always been a curse.

"Yes, I'm going to Boston."

"Can I share your car?"

"Oh. No. I don't think that's a good idea. I'm sure you'll find a car at another agency."

I kept walking when I felt her hand grab my arm.

She begged me.

She stood there—a damsel in distress—and I had no desire to help her in any way. That was terrible. I knew that. But she was such a pain.

"I promised my little son that I'd be home for his birthday."

Oh, for pity's sake.

Half of me—more than half of me—figured I was being conned. The odds were she had no child at all. The odds were I'd do all the driving and she'd find some way to not chip in for the cost of the car. The odds were it would be a long miserable ride and I'd be a fool to agree.

"Sure," I said. "Sure. We'll get you home for your son's birthday."

She smiled. I didn't believe the smile. But I smiled back.

Her name was Claire Tremaine and she said—she claimed—that she lived in Brockton, which is about forty minutes south of Boston. Which meant, round trip, I'd waste an additional hour or more.

It took 14 hours to get her to her house. The snow cost me at least 4 hours.

It wasn't however, such a bad ride—because we discovered that we both loved movies.

She started the game—sort of a game—by asking, "Who said, 'They call me, Mr. Tibbs'?"

"Sidney Poitier," I said. *"In the Heat of the Night."*

She smiled, and I countered with, " 'Frankly, my dear, I don't give a damn.' "

"Oh, come on. That's a baby question. Rhett Butler. Clark Gable. *Gone with the Wind.* 1939. Selznick International Pictures. Directed by Victor Fleming."

We were off and running.

She lowered her voice to a sexy pitch and said, " 'Why don't you come up and see me sometime?' "

"Marilyn Monroe," I said.

"No. Mae West."

" 'You can't handle the truth,' " I ventured.

"A Few Good Men. Jack Nicholson."

"You're good at this," I said.

" 'There's no crying in baseball,' " she said, not giving an inch.

"Oh. I know that."

"If you know it, say it."

"I know it. I know it."

"Stop stalling for time."

"*A League of Their Own*. Tom Hanks."

"Not bad." she said.

" 'I've always relied on the kindness of strangers.' "

She was stumped. I couldn't believe it. When I told her, she said she'd never heard of *A Streetcar Named Desire*.

We kept going. Maybe an hour more. We stopped playing the game and just started talking about scenes we liked.

She loved the *When Harry Met Sally* scene in the diner when Meg Ryan fakes having sex, and a woman seated at another table says to the waiter, "I'll have what she's having."

"You know," I said, "the woman is Rob Reiner's mother—doing a cameo."

"Really?"

"Yep. Okay. Ever see the movie *Nobody's Fool?*" I asked. "The one made in the 80s with Rosanna Arquette—not the one made in the 90s with Paul Newman."

She hadn't seen it, and I talked about the scene where the heroine is telling a guy that she can't go out with him or be happy with her life because she's guilty of doing a terrible thing.

"So, he looks at her—they're driving in a car—and he says something like, 'I once made love to my aunt's live-in nurse, on the cold linoleum bathroom floor, while my aunt was choking to death in the next room. So—what did *you* do?' "

I laughed.

"That's such a great scene. I'll never forget it."

But Claire wasn't laughing.

"What's wrong?" I asked.

She didn't say anything.

"Did I say something to offend you?"

"No. No. Of course not."

"I shouldn't have talked about a sex scene?"

"No. No. Of course not. Don't be silly."

"Oh. Well. Sorry, anyway."

"When I was eighteen, I was going to go to the mall with my sister Pearl. She was fifteen. We were in the car. I was backing out of our driveway. And we were talking—about boys. And I wasn't paying attention. And—I shot out into the street and a car slammed into us. Into Pearl's side of the car. She hit her head hard on the window. Glass shattered. Her face and her eyes were cut. She was knocked out. Blood was pouring down both sides of her face."

Claire started to cry.

"Want me to pull over? Should I get off the highway?"

"No. No."

Claire looked at me and smiled.

"I don't know why I'm telling you this."

"Because I'd like to hear it?"

She told me about going to the hospital. Emergency surgery. Pearl would live. But—she was blind and would remain blind.

"Those beautiful blue eyes. Pearl has the most vibrant blue eyes you've ever seen. They're startling. Beautiful eyes. Beautiful eyes that cannot see."

"Could she see after the accident?"

"No. I told you. She went blind."

"No. I mean right after the accident. Right after the car was hit. Or on the way to the hospital. Could she see?"

"Um. No. Well, I don't know. She was unconscious. I have no idea. Why do you ask?"

"Did the doctors say it was retinal damage? Or nerve damage?"

"I think it was— I'm not sure. I think it was the eye itself. Not the nerve. I don't know. Why do you ask?"

"Oh. Just trying to figure out what happened."

"You said you clean banks for a living?"

"Well. Yes. But I used to be a doctor."

"Used to be?"

"Want to know what I did? I helped a girl kill herself."

I told Claire the story of Linda and the abortion and the suicide.

"That wasn't your fault," Claire said. "She killed herself because of the abortion. It didn't matter who performed the abortion."

"I know that. In my brain, I know that. But in my heart, I know that I was the one who took away her desire to live."

Claire didn't say a word. She sat very still and looked straight ahead. I kept my eye on the road and didn't say anything either.

It seemed like an hour—but it was probably only ten minutes.

Claire started to cry.

"Claire—"

"I'm sorry," she said. "I can't help it. I'm crying—for both of us."

Claire wanted to talk about her sister.

"Pearl is so beautiful. Those eyes! And—and I think this is exceptional—she never blamed me for the accident. For losing her sight."

"Carlos never blamed me," I said. "Well, maybe for ten minutes. We worked it out."

"Same with Pearl," Claire said. "Pearl is so accomplished. You should hear her play the guitar. And she reads all the time. You know, braille. She's read all of Shakespeare. She loves F. Scott Fitzgerald. She's read *The Great Gatsby* like ten times."

So we drove on. Through the snow. Through the darkness.

Through our lives.

This woman, who I didn't think I could stand being with for five minutes, kept my interest for fourteen hours.

When we were about three hours away from her home, she called and spoke with her mother. Claire gave all kinds of directions about the birthday cake and where the presents were hidden. How many pizzas to order and what paper plates and napkins to use.

"How are the roads?" she asked. "Will people be able to make the party?"

It had stopped snowing in Brockton. The roads were clear and everyone was expected to arrive.

"Great," Claire said. "And I'm bringing a guest. His name is Tim."

I motioned "No" with my face—but she just waved me off.

"He doesn't want to come. But he's coming."

When she hung up, I knew I was going to the party even though I was going to try and talk my way out of it.

"I'm so tired," I said. "And it's your family. I just want to drop you off—no offense, I've really enjoyed our ride."

"You have some pizza and some cake and then you go home to Boston."

"All right," I said. "You win."

Then I thought, and added, "That didn't sound very gracious on my part. I'm very happy to come to your son's party. Wait. A present. I need a present. How old is he? What's his name?"

"You don't need a present. You're bringing me home to his party. That's present enough. His name is Ben and he's nine."

"Nine. Um— A toy car? A toy truck? A model?"

"You don't have to give him anything."

"I won't stay without a present."

"Okay. Toy cars and trucks? Do you think this is 1960? Give him an iTunes gift certificate. Twenty bucks. You give me a twenty and I'll slip into the study and order one and print it off and you give it to him."

"Good idea."

The last two hours of the drive flew by, because Claire found a great oldies station and started singing along. I joined in on Janis Joplin's *Me and Bobby McGee* and that was that. We sang at the top of our voices right up to her front door.

The party was most likely a lot of fun. I don't remember any of it.

That's because, when we walked into the living room, Claire took me right up to her sister Pearl and took my hand and put it in Pearl's hand and said, "Pearl, I want you to meet your future husband, you ugly witch."

CHAPTER SIXTEEN
Pearl

You find yourself saying the word "see" to blind people a lot, and then you find yourself apologizing a lot.

"See" is a very common word.

"*See* what I mean?"

"*See* the little action figures on top of the cake."

"You won't believe it unless you *see* it."

I'm sorry. I'm sorry. I'm sorry.

"If you're going to be my husband," Pearl said after about an hour of small talk—punctuated by my apologies, "you have to stop apologizing all the time. In fact, you have to stop apologizing, period. Unless, of course, you do something rotten to me and then, naturally, you'd better apologize."

"I would never do anything rotten to you," I countered.

"Time will tell."

"Do I have some time? With you?" I ventured.

"I have all the time in the world."

"So—you're not—you know—attached or anything?"

82

"Who'd get himself attached to a blind girl?" she said.

"A really ugly man," I said.

That might not have been such a good thing to say.

I held my breath.

"You're not ugly," Pearl said. "I can tell."

"Don't you have to—you know—feel my face with your hands? I've seen that in movies."

"Movies about blind people?"

"You don't give a guy a break, do you?" I said.

Then I leaned forward and kissed her on the cheek.

"That the best you can do?" she said.

"Well. Your whole family is here. And you're blind."

"I am?"

"So—you know—kissing a blind girl might be construed as taking advantage. You know. Of the blind girl."

This was getting me nowhere.

I leaned in a bit and whispered in her ear, "This time she just might be right."

Pearl looked at me. It is okay to say *look*—as in point your eyes at someone. Pearl didn't see me, but she did indeed look at me.

"What do you mean?" she whispered.

I bent over again and quietly said, "Your sister Claire. She's right. I am going to be your husband."

I have never, never in my life, seen anything as beautiful as those blue eyes. Pearl smiled and her eyes lit up. The eyes were blank. But they somehow managed to light up nonetheless. It was as if by magic.

I was gone the moment I saw her. Head over heels gone. It wasn't sympathy. It wasn't the fourteen-hour drive.

What it was—was that when I looked at Pearl, I saw kindness.

I didn't drive home. I stayed really late and then called the Brockton Arms and got a room—against everyone's protestations, as they wanted me to stay there. But I wanted to establish neutrality. I wanted to have my own base.

"You wanted your stinking autonomy," Marisol said to me later on when I saw her and told her the story.

So after 11:00 P.M., I said my goodbyes and kissed Pearl on the cheek again and walked out to my car.

The snow had started up again. But it was nothing. Nothing compared to what we had driven through.

I opened the door and was about to get in when I felt a hand on my arm.

I turned.

It was Pearl.

It was very dark—even with the moonlight bouncing off of the snow—but Pearl's eyes flashed at me.

"A kiss on the cheek may be quite continental—"

"*Diamonds are a Girl's Best Friend,*" I said. "Marilyn Monroe."

"Claire said you were good."

I leaned over and kissed her on the mouth and pulled her toward me.

She threw her arms around me and kissed me like there was no tomorrow.

I had to go. I had to establish my neutrality.

I touched her face and watched as she scampered back inside the house—marveling at how she maneuvered with ease.

I had no idea how she did it.

I knew only one thing right then and there.

There would be many tomorrows.

CHAPTER SEVENTEEN
The First Good Thing

Totally blind, Pearl saw more than most people. Incredibly, she loved me as much as I loved her.

I stayed at the Brockton Arms for two days. Each morning, I showed up at Pearl's house with coffee and the best bagels ever—that I found in a small Portuguese bakery in Stoughton. Pearl and I would sit in the living room, by the old-fashioned bay window and have coffee and eat fresh bagels with cream cheese. Not toasted. Just fresh—as is—with cold cream cheese slathered all over them.

And really hot coffee.

One thing we found that we instantly had in common was coffee.

"I need at least six cups of coffee in the morning," I told her.

"Six? I need six cups just to get my heart started."

"You get my heart started," I said. "Every time I see you."

"I want you to take me for coffee," she said.

"What do you mean? Different coffee?"

She took my cup and put it down and then put her arms around me and kissed me.

"Touch me," she said.

I thought my life was starting over. Nothing that had happened mattered. Only Pearl mattered.

"Take me for coffee," she said. "To New York. I understand that they have great coffee in New York."

We were in the car in minutes.

I probably owed Avis thousands of dollars for the Mustang by now. I could not have cared less.

I drove straight to Times Square and turned up on Seventh and got to the Plaza.

"You're where?" Todd asked me when I called.

"I'm at the Plaza."

"In New York?"

"Of course."

"Why are you at the Plaza? Why are you in New York?"

"I'm with Pearl."

"Who's Pearl?"

"The girl I love."

"Okay— Do you want to tell me this from the beginning?"

"Well, let's begin with the simple fact that Pearl is the first good thing that's happened to me in all the years I can remember."

"Say no more," Todd said. "See you when you get home."

"Thanks," I said.

When I hung up, Pearl came out of the bathroom.

"This room is great. You should see the robes in the bathroom. It's a good thing too."

"Why?"

"We didn't bring any clothes. We didn't pack."

"I'll take you shopping."

"Really? Shopping? Now?"

"No? Not now?"

"You can take me shopping if you want. Sure. Take me shopping. After you take me to bed."

Her jet-black hair. Her porcelain-white skin. Her angel eyes the color of the sky on a perfect summer day.

We loved each other and showed each other how much we loved.

We went shopping. We went to a show. We went to Central Park. We went to the opera.

But we always went back to bed.

When we left New York, we drove straight to Marisol's house and Pearl moved in.

A minute after I introduced her, she was part of our family.

"Pearl, dear," Marisol said, "I've never had another woman in this house. Just me and the boys. I'm so glad you're here."

"You're as beautiful as Tim said you are," Pearl replied.

"How—?"

Marisol caught herself.

"Oh, don't you start apologizing too," Pearl said.

"I never apologize," Marisol said.

"Neither do I."

"Of course not. You had your eyes taken. I had my son taken."

"Do you have the strength, Marisol, to let it go?" Pearl asked.

"I have to," Marisol answered. "For me, there is no other choice."

"That's good," Pearl said.

"Why?" Marisol asked.

"When you find the strength to let it go," Pearl said, "you never have to look back again."

"Oh, I look back. But I only look back at little Martinez. I look back at him every day. But I live forward."

"As do I," Pearl said. "As do I."

A month later, Pearl and I were married. It was a small civil ceremony in Marisol's house.

Pearl was more beautiful than any woman had a right to be.

Marisol handled everything, and everything was perfect.

Todd and Carlos teamed up to be best men. And Claire, good old Claire, was Pearl's matron of honor.

Pearl and I took off for another week in New York. I got the same room at the Plaza and we did everything we could think of. And we could think of a lot of things to do.

When we got back, I threw myself into BankJob—because I had let my responsibilities go and had to get things righted again.

The Alonzos were gang busters. So much so that we hired more of them. Six Alonzo cousins joined the team. New banks signed up. Business was good. In fact, business was great.

We were planning a party for our second anniversary of starting the business. Todd found a great barbecue place that made the best ribs and pulled pork. Steak fries. Cold beer. It would have been a lot of fun. It would have been a milestone.

It was a milestone, as things turned out.

Just not the kind that any of us ever imagined.

CHAPTER EIGHTEEN
It Makes You Wonder

My mother and father lost their lives because of a rebuilt gascolater fuel-bowl assembly.

Marisol lost her son because she took a moment to place a seashell on top of a sandcastle.

Carlos lost Linda because I did something I knew was wrong.

All of us lost every penny we had because of a man who simply said he was our friend.

Now it was a garbage bag.

Juanita Alonzo had a habit of counting out the trash-can liners for each room as she cleaned it. She'd stand in the middle of the room and, with her finger, point to each trash can and count it out silently, but mouthing the words.

The back office of the Iron Street branch of Boston United Savings Bank had six trash cans. Juanita verified this with her silent count and then licked her fingers for traction and peeled off six liners—counting as she went, "One, two, three, four, five, six."

I assume she counted in Spanish, but of course that really doesn't matter.

In a moment of unusual inattention, she placed all but one liner on top of a desk and then turned around to empty one can and replace the liner. As she turned, two of the liners she had left on top of the desk slid off and fell to the floor.

Silently, of course. She had no idea.

Juanita turned around and walked toward the desk. Of course she slipped on the plastic liners that were on the floor.

She could have walked the other way around the desk. She could have looked down and said something like, "Oh, silly me. These must have fallen."

But she didn't. She tread right on top of the liners and—as there was no purchase—her feet flew out from under her. She smashed her head on the edge of one desk and her back against the corner of an-other desk.

There.

In the blink of an eye.

In the time it took the gascolater fuel-bowl assembly to fail, in the time it took Marisol to reach up and put a shell on a tower of sand, in the time it took Linda to open a window.

In a span of time too small to bother measuring, Juanita Alonzo was the unwitting mechanism that once again took everything we had.

"I think she fell on purpose," Carlos said. "Why not? Think of the money."

"Carlos," Marisol said, "if she fell on purpose she would have planned it so that she didn't break her—her what, Timothy?"

"Her spinal cord. Well, it's not broken. It's damaged. There's a chance—a slim chance, but a chance—that she could walk again. Someday."

The court case started about six months later and lasted a mere three days. Sure, Juanita dropped the liners herself. Sure, Juanita fell herself. How could it possibly be our fault?

Twelve million dollars.

That was her award.

Twelve million dollars.

Our lawyer was very good and presented all of the evidence in a clear and precise manner. But Juanita's team of lawyers put on a three-ring circus and so dazzled the jury that they tripped over themselves giving away our money.

Everything came out. The judge allowed everything, because Juanita's lawyers passionately and successfully argued that their client's case centered on us having a history of bad business decisions.

I had lost my medical license.

Carlos had lost his job.

Todd's company had gone bust.

Juanita's lawyers argued that we were three men who always generated disastrous outcomes.

The jury bought it.

Our insurance company agreed to pay three million, as our policy dictated. That left us holding a nine-million-dollar bag.

So we struck a deal with Juanita's lawyers.

They gave us eight months to come up with more money; if we couldn't, then Juanita got our company—lock, stock and barrel.

I never knew what the "barrel" meant in that saying. But it was a barrel they had us over and there was nothing we could do about it.

An appeal was pointless, our lawyer maintained. So did the insurance-company lawyer. It would cost another small fortune—and we'd lose again.

It was a done deal and that's all there was to it.

The jury held to one simple idea: Juanita would probably never walk and we were three Harvard grads who had every opportunity in the world and seemed to have a penchant for throwing everything away.

We couldn't even fire the remaining Alonzos—Hermann and Luis, plus the new band of Alonzo cousins we had brought on board to bolster our work force. They all dutifully came to work each evening.

Pearl figured it out.

"It's really simple," she said one night a few weeks after the verdict, when all of us were eating dinner. "They know we will never come up with the other nine million dollars. So, they know they're going to get the business and they want to keep it running at full speed until they do."

"I see," Marisol said.

"I don't," Pearl shot out and then laughed.

We laughed even though there was nothing funny to laugh about.

"It makes you wonder, doesn't it?" Todd said.

"What do you mean?" I asked.

"The whole thing. The bank just happened to be Boston United Savings Bank. We have eleven banks under contract—and that's the one where it happened? And why didn't Juanita sue the bank? Why weren't they included? You always go after the deep pockets. But they didn't. They just went after us."

"You think something was going on?" Todd asked.

"It makes you wonder."

"I don't wonder," Marisol said. "It's Shel Crummins. Crummy Pig Bastardo. It's that bank. Curse the day we ever met him and curse the day we ever met that bank."

None of us said anything. None of us said the usual, "Oh, come on, Mom. Don't be silly."

Pearl broke the silence.

"I'm sure Marisol is right."

Of course she was right. The bank wanted us to go away. It was impossible to think that Shel Crummins had acted alone. It was impossible to think that the bank had no idea what he was up to.

Then we were sued and screwed and the bank saw the lawsuit as a way to bury us—and, although we could prove nothing, we knew that it was in their very best interest for us to lose

"How could the three of us who are—you know, essentially brilliant—not see this happening?" Todd asked.

"Because you're too smart," Marisol said. "You see all the trees. You know the names of each tree. In Latin. You know how each tree grows. You know what each tree is worth. You know how many trees there are. You know more about each tree than anyone could possibly know."

"But," I said, "we don't see the forest."

"No," Marisol said, "you see the forest all right. You see the streams. You see the lake. You see everything. What you don't see is the people in the forest. You don't see how bad some of them are."

"That's what I love about Tim," Pearl said. "That's what I love about all of you. It's better to have an open heart."

Then Pearl turned to Marisol and said, "I wish I could see a tree."

Marisol's mouth opened wide.

Pearl laughed.

We all laughed.

Marisol tried to say something, but couldn't get any words out over the laughter.

Finally, Marisol gained some control over herself and said, "You know— You know what would be— You know what would be funny? If— If— If you robbed the bank."

We stopped laughing.

CHAPTER NINETEEN
You Need a Plan

"Why not?" Marisol asked.

"Well, how about because it's wrong and we're not criminals," I answered.

"Technically—you are a criminal," Todd said.

This brought out another round of laughter.

I looked at Carlos—I felt terrible.

"There's nothing to say," Carlos said. "We've been through this. I'm not going to hit you again. I'm not going to scream at you again. I'm not going to hit anything or scream at anyone or do anything again about Linda."

"So—?" Marisol said.

"What?" Carlos asked.

"So—let's rob the bank."

"I can be the lookout," Pearl said.

We couldn't laugh any more.

"Or the hear-out. Or the smell-out."

She moved her head in a sweeping motion, as if she could see us.

"You still there? Or have you all sneaked out of the room? I was joking, naturally. This is all a joke. Right? Right, Marisol?"

"Is what Shel Crummins did a joke? Is what Juanita did a joke? Is what the bank did a joke?" Marisol replied.

"We don't know for sure that the bank itself had anything to do with any of this," I threw out.

"Of course they did!" Todd said, slamming his hand down on the table.

We all flinched.

"I didn't see that coming," Pearl said.

"Pearl—"

"I've got a million of them," she said.

"And we have heard them all," I said.

No one said anything for a moment.

"We can't do anything about the people we've lost," Todd said. "And we can't blame anyone for that. Life happens. But—and I know the money isn't important in the grand scheme of life— How any of us would trade all that we had to get—"

He stopped.

"To get Mom and Dad back?" I said.

"To get Linda back," Carlos said.

"To get Martinez back," Marisol said.

"To get my sight back," Pearl said.

"Right," Todd said. "Exactly. We'd trade it all in a heartbeat. That's obvious. So in that sense, the money doesn't really matter. But—in another sense—when they took all of our money, they took away our livelihood. They took away our sustenance. It would be like we were farmers and the bank took our farm. It's not just the income that you'd lose—it's your very way of living. Sure, we can muddle on. Sure, we can give the business over to the Alonzo clan and still survive. Sure, we can sell this house—the one thing we have left. We can have it all taken away and we can find a way to go on. But—they took it from us. They took it."

"Why not take it back?" Carlos said.

"I broke the law once—" I said, and then stopped talking.

All eyes turned in my direction.

"Timothy—?" Marisol said.

"I broke the law once," I began again. "My back was to the wall. If I hadn't done it, Linda would have sought out someone who would have done it. I broke the law, but I broke the law to save her. And we know how that turned out. If we break the law now, the world will judge us just as harshly. Our defense can't be that we were cheated. We live in a country of laws. If we were cheated we should go to the courts. But the courts won't help us because we can't prove a thing. Maybe if we spent years and years—and hired lawyers and detectives. But we don't have the time and we don't have the money. So if we took—matters—into our own hands, we'd have to leave. We'd have to go somewhere. Because the world would be against us. We could never get away with it—scot-free. What do you do with the money? How do people who've lost everything—lost everything in a well-documented public way—how do those people buy a home and buy food and buy cars and live a normal life—if they supposedly have no money? Not to mention that if they thought we had money, they'd come after us to pay off the Alonzos. It's a circle that gets smaller and smaller around us. I think the bank knew this. I think they knew that if we lost the court case to the Alonzos—which we did—then we'd spend the rest of our lives just trying to breathe inside that ever-smaller circle. They knew that. They knew about what Shel did. They knew about what the Alonzos did. They pushed us into the circle and let it shrink around us. They've known every step of the way what they were doing. And then did it willingly and gleefully. And they're in their plush offices—looking out their wall-to-wall windows—knowing that they have just that much more money in their vaults and there's not one blessed thing we can do about it. Well—not one blessed thing that we can do that they'd ever *expect* us to do."

I looked at all of them.

"I broke the law once," I said. "I have nothing to lose by breaking the law again."

It was said and done.

Marisol stood up from the table.

"Let us all go and think. And let us come back to this table tomorrow night for dinner. I will make *paella*. And we will make a plan."

She walked out of the room like the Queen of the Mist.

Silence.

"If," Pearl said at length, "you give me a braille map—I'll drive the getaway car."

CHAPTER TWENTY
Paella

The paella was the best ever. Marisol outdid herself. During dinner, we didn't talk of banks and vaults and getaway vans.

After dinner, after the dishes were cleared and the table wiped down, we each got a new Corona Extra with a lime slice at the top like a flag.

I pushed my lime slice in immediately. Marisol rubbed the slice around and around the inside of the bottle's neck. Pearl took the slice and ate it. Skin and all.

There is nothing like the first sip of a really cold Corona.

"Well," I said. "I guess we should talk. It's been a whole day now and I think we've probably all come to our senses and—"

"I have no problem with you boys opening the vault," Marisol said. "I'm sure you can do it. My problem is how to get the money out of the country."

"What?" I said. "No. Wait. We've had a day. I'm sure everyone—"

"Getting the money out of the vault is the easy part," Carlos said. "You're right. It's getting the money out of the country that is the hard part."

"Why is the vault the easy part?" Marisol asked. "Because you're math whizzes you think you can open the safe? How? Cal-ku-loose?"

"Calculus," Carlos said.

"Excuse me for living," Marisol said. "Excuse me for being your mother and sending you to fancy schools. Excuse me for—"

"Sorry, Mom. Sorry. I'm just excited. I know how to do it."

"That's okay, my Carlos. I knew you'd figure it all out. Using the math in your brain."

"Well, not so much math. But we are going to use computers and algorithms and off-shore servers—and we have to change some clocks. And then—"

"Wait!" I shouted. "Just stop a minute."

"I can't stop," Carlos said. "I figured it all out. It seemed impossible at first. But once I got into it—it was really quite simple."

"But—we're not going to rob the bank. We're not criminals."

"Last night," Todd chimed in, "you made the speech that sealed the deal."

"That was last night. The spirit of the moment. I've had time to think. We're not criminals. Not even me. We're not bank robbers."

"So—you are against this?" Marisol asked.

"I'm—against robbing a bank. I'm not against us."

"I don't think there is a difference, Timothy."

Pearl reached out and touched my hand and then leaned over and whispered to me, "I have to talk to you in private."

She got up and walked away from the table into the kitchen.

I followed her.

"What's up?" I asked. "This is crazy, isn't it?"

"Did you see Carlos? Did you see how excited he is? He's been like that all day. You were out at work, but Carlos stayed here. He worked like a madman. He was scribbling reams in one of those marble notebooks you guys like. Well, I assume it was one of those marble notebooks. But I could hear him writing. And writing. And writing. Then he got on the computer in the kitchen—I heard that too—and he made a big pot of coffee and he drank coffee and typed away furiously."

"So?"

"So? By what you've told me, this is the first time since Linda died that he's shown any interest in anything. You told me he lost his job because he couldn't bring himself to concentrate on work. Since I've known him I've barely spoken more than a sentence a day to him. Now. All of a sudden. He's alive with energy."

"So you think we should rob a bank—commit this gigantic felony—put our freedom in jeopardy—not to mention live the rest of our lives on the run—just because Carlos is having fun?"

"Yes."

"That's nuts."

"You owe him that."

I was stunned.

"You can't blame me for Linda. That wasn't my fault."

"You broke the law. You did something illegal and unethical. And Linda died. Maybe those two things aren't connected. Maybe she would have jumped out of that window even if she had gone to the best hospital in the world. Maybe she would have. And that thought will let you sleep at night. But—the simple fact of the matter is: You broke the law and Linda jumped out of the window."

I stared at her and took a long sip of my Corona.

"Do you blame Claire for what happened to you?"

"Of course I blame Claire! She was driving. It was 100 percent her fault. Of course I blame her. I forgave her. I forgave her back then right after it happened. There was no doubt that I would forgive her. She's my sister and she loves me and I love her. Of course I forgave her. But it was still all her fault."

"But—okay—I see the change in Carlos. It's great to see him—passionate again. But—this is breaking the law. This is stealing what doesn't belong to us."

"Forget the law. It's not a question of the law. Of course it's breaking the law. But that's trumped by the fact that the bank stole your money. You're stealing back what they stole from you. And—"

She held up her hand to silence my oncoming refutal of what she was saying.

"And—sure—two wrongs don't make a right. But— you can't make it right. You said it yourself. You have no recourse. They hold all the cards. They're gloating in their victory. Because they know there's nothing you can do. Except—didn't you say this last night?—except if you do something no one on this earth would expect you to do."

She kissed me suddenly on the lips. Full and hard.

"Besides," she said, "I've always had a thing for bandits."

CHAPTER TWENTY-ONE
Carlos

"We're in," I said.

Pearl and I had walked back to the dinner table.

"We're in. We're in all the way. Carlos—what's the plan?"

He was passionate. He was enthused. He could hardly get it all out for all the energy he was expelling from his body.

Carlos walked around and around the table. He held up sheets of paper with crazy mathematical hieroglyphics. He had a flow chart with little boxes and little circles and little triangles. The triangles, apparently, were key.

The chart was color coded. Red and blue mostly. But the triangles were bright yellow. And the triangles were key.

"The triangles are key," Carlos said. "They control everything."

Our buddy the master math whiz was now a master criminal whiz.

Getting into the bank was the easy part. We were in the bank at night and we were supposed to be there. So there was no problem with entry.

When to do it took some figuring. Carlos knew that the Iron Street Branch of Boston United Savings Bank was a depository of the Federal Reserve. That part was common knowledge. But when would there be the most money in the vault? Carlos had spent hours the day before—he hadn't slept at all and worked all through the night—so that when Pearl realized he was making a huge pot of coffee it wasn't Carlos starting his work, it was Carlos finishing his work. He had done the bulk of the planning—the bulk of the research the night before. In the long hours of the late night and of the early morning, Carlos had used public records to determine that the Iron Street Branch of the Boston United Savings Bank got a Federal Reserve deposit on the seventeenth of every third month.

"It only stays in the bank for one day. Then it's loaded up and shipped out via armored cars to banks all over Massachusetts, Rhode Island and Connecticut. So there is a small window. But—see this yellow triangle over here?—that's the one. That's the day it will work. Because that day is the only seventeenth of the month—counting ahead every three months—that falls on a Saturday. The money will be delivered on a Saturday morning. But it won't leave until Monday morning. That's the key. See it? Do you see it? If we take the money Saturday night—say at eleven o'clock at night—that gives us until nine o'clock Monday morning until the discovery is made. That gives us—"

"Thirty-four hours," Pearl said.

"Exactly!" Carlos said, a huge smile coming over his face. "That gives us thirty-four hours to open the vault, take the money, put it all in one of our vans and drive to Belize."

"Belize?" I said. "Belize?"

"Belize is the place. Want to know why?"

"No," Marisol said. "What I want to know is—on the seventeenth of that month—when all the money is put into the vault—how much money will there be?"

"Oh," Carlos said. "Let me see. Let me see. It's in one of these blue squares—or is it in a red circle?"

"Carlos. I do not care about the circles and the squares or even about your precious triangles. How much money?"

"It's right here. Here it is."

He looked up at us and then looked down at his flow chart and then looked up again.

"Thirty-nine million dollars. Approximately."

"Thirty-nine million—"

"Approximately," he said. "It varies. But thirty-nine million is a very good approximation. I'd be surprised if it were more than a million off in either direction."

He looked down at his chart and then looked up at us again.

"Yep. Thirty-nine million. Dollars. Approximately."

CHAPTER TWENTY-TWO
Belize

Carlos looked at us. As if to say, "Well?"

Pearl spoke up first.

"Thirty-nine million dollars seems like enough," she said. "I mean—you're the ones that lost all the money. Not me. But it would seem to me that thirty-nine million dollars would do the trick."

"Approximately," Carlos added.

"Stop with the approximately," Marisol shouted. "I'm happy with a million. I'm very happy with ten million."

"But it is approximately thirty-nine million. I'm sure of it."

Marisol looked at her son and shook her head.

"You are a very smart boy, Carlos. I am very proud of you."

"Thanks, Mom."

"Now—tell us, my Carlos—why in the world would we go to Belize? Where is Belize? Would I like Belize?"

"You'd love Belize!" Carlos shouted. "Look, on this page, I have a map. Belize is in Central America. It borders Mexico on its north. It borders Guatemala on its west and south."

"And what about on its East?" Marisol asked.

"On the east, is the Caribbean Sea."

"I like that," Marisol said, a huge smile coming over her face.

"Listen," Carlos said. "Belize is the place. They speak English. It's an independent country. But Queen Elizabeth is their queen. It's weird. I never understand this whole United Kingdom thing. But it's essentially an independent country. The population is less than 400,000. And the whole country is less than 9,000 square miles. The whole country is smaller than New Hampshire."

"I do not like New Hampshire," Marisol shouted out. "Too cold for me."

"Well Belize is nice and warm all year round. And—it gets better! Listen to this. Their motto—the country has a motto—their motto is: *Under the shade I flourish.* Isn't that great! The national pastime is sitting under the shade. We can do that. And—and—when they're not playing *God Save the Queen*, their own anthem is called *Land of the Free*. It's like us. Land of the Free. Home of the Brave. And—Belize is the birthplace of chewing gum!"

"Oh, I do not like chewing gum," Marisol said. "I think that women who chew gum are cheap. I don't care what you may think. It's cheap. All that smacking of the jaws and the lips sucking in and out. Men don't marry women who chew gum."

"Notwithstanding that, Mom, they also drive on the right! On the right! I tell you it's the perfect place."

He smiled.

"Oh, I forgot. They don't have an extradition treaty with us. Well, they do. But it's new and it's never been used—and it does cover things like robbery—but, in reality—it's really for terrorists. And think about it—it's Belize. They don't care. Once we get there, we're there."

"Can we ever come back?" Pearl asked.

"Not right away. We could come back after the statute of limitations expires."

"Six years?" Pearl asked.

"Yes. Well. No. Well—it depends. It's five years. Unless—and this is key—we were indicted before the five years were up. So—if they don't indict us for five years, then we're free and clear. So, if we do it right, they'd have no real evidence to indict us. I mean—they'll probably figure out that it had to be us—but they'd have to have some proof to indict us. We can't worry about that."

"Well, I worry about it. My family is here."

I patted Pearl's hand.

"We can call it off, right now," I said.

"Oh. Honey. Thanks so much."

She kissed me and then said to everyone, "We can fly them down all the time, right?"

"Of course we can," Carlos said. "It's a wonderful place to visit. We'll be right on the ocean. Oh! Listen to this! We're going down the east coast, almost all the way down to the border with Guatemala. Right on the coast. We're going to live right on the coast. In a town called New Haven. Get it? Isn't that great?"

We all looked at him.

"Don't you get it? We all went to Harvard. And we're going to live in New Haven."

Carlos looked at Marisol.

"Yale is in New Haven," he said.

"Oh," she said. "And we hate the Yale school, right?"

"More or less."

"New Haven is on the sea. Right on the sea. Oh. And there are monkeys. Howler monkeys. Belize has lots of monkeys. Spider monkeys too."

"Wait—" I said. "Did you say howler monkeys?"

"Yeah. Why?"

"Oh. Nothing. I've read about them. Interesting species."

"I like the monkeys," Marisol said. "I don't want the monkeys touching me. But I like to look at them."

Marisol stopped for a moment.

Then she looked at Todd and said, "Todd. You haven't said a word. Do you not think this is a good plan?"

Todd started to speak. Then stopped. Then he looked at Carlos and said, "I haven't heard a plan yet. We know the *who*, the *what*, the *why*, the *where* and the *when*. But—you haven't said *how* we get the money. *How* do we open the vault? How in the world do we open the vault?"

Marisol was about to jump in—but Carlos held up his hand to divert her.

"I already said that opening the vault is easy. All we have to do is hack into the website that controls the atomic clock."

"That's all," Todd said.

"Well, no. I'm being a tad dramatic."

"Just a tad?" I ventured.

Carlos gave me a look.

110

"We're not going to hack the National Institute of Standards," he said. "We probably could, but that would be hard. All we're going to do is hack the site of Falmouth Air."

"Falmouth Air?" Todd asked.

"It's a very small airline. In Falmouth. You know, on the Cape."

"I know where Falmouth is."

"They have an airport?" Marisol asked.

"A tiny airport with only one runway. Which is okay, because they have only one plane. It's a Cessna. This gets stranger and stranger. There's a lot of things that could be construed as omens in this plan. But I don't know if they're good omens or bad omens. I found it by luck, so that might mean something. I was looking for transportation companies that had revenue of less than two hundred thousand dollars a year. I figured small is stupid. Which, in this instance, turned out to be accurate."

"What has the airport got to do with the bank?" I asked.

"Well, nothing at all. Except—"

Carlos paused.

"This is the crux of the matter. It came to me after my twelfth cup of coffee this morning."

"You drank the entire pot yourself?" Pearl asked.

"Three pots."

"And," Todd threw in, "we're going to trust a guy on a caffeine high?"

"Check it out for yourself," he said.

Carlos opened a laptop and spread it out before us.

"Look. Here's the site for Falmouth Air. Now look. We open the source code. See. See right there. On the seventh line down."

"I see nothing I understand," Marisol said.

"That's more than I see," Pearl said.

"Pearl—you must stop yourself from saying these things all the time."

"Can we concentrate on the source code," Carlos sort of yelled. "Look. These lines. These four lines get the time. The time has to be accurate for scheduling. It's all required by the FCC. Airlines. Trains. Buses. All transportation. All transportation has to be working on the same clock or there would be disasters."

"I remember dad's pocket watch," I said. "it was a Waltham. 1876. A train-conductor's watch."

"I remember that," Todd said. "He'd show us how it was wound and how the conductors had to synchronize the time."

"Otherwise trains would crash into each other," I added.

"That's right," Carlos said. "That's it exactly. So—every airline has to have the correct time. And they get it from an internet hook-up with the National Institute of Standards."

"So?" Todd said.

"So. Look at this source code for time. It's not encrypted. We can hack in—you know—if you know what to do and have no scruples—"

"Which is you, my Carlos."

"That's me, Mom. It's not encrypted. Not at all. They must have not known what they were doing when they set this up. But Falmouth Air is a fly-by-night—no pun intended—airline. Run by two brothers. Twins! Like us! Only stupid twins. One is the pilot. The other runs the

112

business. So all I have to do is hack into their site and change the time."

"Wait," Pearl yelled. "If you change the time, then all the trains will crash all over the country."

"That would not be a good thing, my Carlos."

"No. No. No. It's more complicated than that. All I do is change the time for Falmouth Air. And I do it at eleven o'clock at night. They don't fly at night. And then I change it back. It won't affect them at all. They'll never know."

"How," Todd said, "does that open the vault?"

"Don't you think I've figured that out? That's the whole crux of the plan. Don't you think I've figured it out?"

"Of course you have, my Carlos."

"Thanks, Mom."

"But we just want to know if it makes sense. You know."

"Sure it makes sense! Would I be standing here showing all of you all of this if it didn't make sense?"

"Carlos," Todd said, "this is not a math-team competition. This is real. How are you going to open the vault?"

Carlos typed something on the laptop and the site came up for Boston United Savings Bank. Then he clicked again, and went to the site for the Iron Street Branch.

"This wouldn't work if they didn't have a separate page for each branch. But they do!"

"Lucky us," Marisol said.

"So. On the night we do it—the seventeenth of May—a Saturday night—we go in like we're cleaning the bank. All of us. We wear coveralls. It won't be a scheduled clean on our calendar. So the Alonzos and all their entourage won't know anything."

"Won't the bank be suspicious?" I asked.

"We're not telling them anything. We're just showing up."

"But the security guard?"

"We tell him that this is one of our bonus cleanings. An extra one we threw in. Like we've done lots of times in the past. And if he asks how come we're there—and where are the Alonzos—we say that we're breaking in some new people and wanted to train them ourselves."

"The new people," Pearl said, "would be Marisol and me?"

"Yes."

"I see," she said.

"Stop it!" Marisol growled.

"Anyway—" Carlos continued, "we go inside. We start cleaning. The guard will be there until 10:45 P.M. Then he leaves for the Spruce Street branch. Then the Tremont Street branch. Then the Dartmouth Street branch. Then he comes back to Iron Street."

"How long does that take him?" I asked.

"One hour and twenty-five minutes. But—we give it a cushion and we plan on one hour. In that one hour we open the vault, take all the money and stuff it very neatly into pockets sewn on the inside of our coveralls. We do this inside the vault."

Carlos looked at us.

"We do this inside the vault," he said, "because there are no security cameras inside the vault. So we kneel on the floor in front of the bins that have all the money from the Federal Reserve. And we take the money—which is, conveniently, wrapped in packets with paper bands—and we place all of the packets inside the pockets that we've sewn on the inside of our coveralls. Then we slip out of the vault and close the door and get back to work until the guard returns. He should get back right after midnight, at about 12:10 A.M. He'll stay until 12:30 A.M. Then he goes off on his rounds to those other banks again. Five minutes after he leaves, we leave. Which makes sense from a cleaning perspective. We'd normally be done by then. We climb into the van and off we go!"

"Into the wild blue yonder," Pearl said.

"But," Carlos went on, "we don't just throw the money into the back of the van. No. Not at all. We put the money under the floor boards."

"Vans have floor boards?" Todd asked.

"Of course the vans have these floor boards," Marisol threw out. "Carlos would know that."

"Vans don't have floor boards," Carlos said. "Nope. Just metal floors. Nothing to lift up. No space to put the money into."

"But you said—?" Marisol started to say.

"But—" Carlos added, "our van will have floor boards. We're going to build an elevated area—it only has to be three-and-a-half inches deep. That's all we need."

"Who will do this for us? Pearl asked. "Won't that be a problem? They could tell the police."

"We will do it ourselves," Carlos answered.

"We can't—"

115

"Yes, we can," Carlos said. "I took metal shop at Stanton. Remember that one term when we were sophomores, when they wanted us to do things that were related to the real world? I took metal shop at a factory in Fall River. It was an internship. I know how to do sheet metal. It's easy."

"Are you sure?" I asked.

"I'll get to that in a bit," Carlos said. "But, yes. I'm sure."

"Won't that be suspicious?" I said. "You know. If we get stopped."

"Of course it will."

"We will not be stopped," Marisol said.

"Oh. We will be stopped. At the border, certainly. But it won't be a problem at all. Well, naturally, anything can be a problem. I mean you can't figure out every single contingency in advance—"

"Carlos—" Marisol said.

Carlos took a breath.

"All along the rim of the back of the van—the outside perimeter of the floor, as it were, there are slots and holes and places for storing tools and what not. But none of them touch the floor. So. We will build a sheet-metal floor above the actual floor. It will be screwed in. Well— not screwed in, in actuality."

"Won't it be all shiny and new looking?" I asked. "Won't that be a give-away?"

"It would be," Carlos said. "But for the fact that I am going to stress the metal in advance. I'll pour acid over it. I'll spill oil and gunk all over it. I'll scrape off the oil and the gunk. Then I'll do it a couple more times. It will look old and worn."

"But the screws—"

"I will not buy galvanized screws. I will buy plain steel screws that are uncoated. They will rust. I will wet them and leave them out and they will rust in two weeks. Then I will drill holes into the new floor and put in the rusty screws—and—this is a nice touch—I will use a very good resin glue to glue the screws into the floor. In that way—in that way—if someone were to try and take a screw out—even with a power drill—they wouldn't budge. It will look to the world as if this floor is old and beaten up and rusted."

"How will we unscrew it to hide the money?" Todd asked.

"We won't unscrew it," Carlos said. "That's what I said before. Let me explain. The screws don't go into anything. They're just for show. The floor will be held in place by powerful electromagnets—run by nine-volt batteries. There will be one on-off switch for the whole system. A small button under the back seat. When I push the button the magnets will shut off and the new floor can easily be lifted up."

We nodded in appreciation.

"But—"

This was Pearl.

"But if you don't need the screws to do anything, then why not just use the magnets and not bother with the screws?"

"This is a thing to think about," Marisol said.

"I've thought about it already," Carlos answered. "If there were no screws, then there would be a seam. You need a seam down the middle because otherwise the floor would be one giant piece and would be very difficult to lift up without getting outside the van and we don't want to be outside the van where we can be seen by parking-lot security cameras lifting up a floor. So you need the floor to be in two sec-

117

tions. That way we can stand on one side and put money into the other side and then reverse the process. So we need a seam. And to prevent anyone from trying to pry up the floor at the seam—we put in fake screws that look like they've been there since the ice age. Or at least ten years."

We nodded again.

"Is there anything you haven't thought of, my Carlos?" Marisol asked in amazement.

"Let's hope not."

"Why, my Carlos?"

"Oh, Because then we'd be caught and we'd go to jail."

We nodded for a third time.

"Of course, we don't put the money under the floor in the bank parking lot," Carlos said.

He waited for some reaction.

"Are you going to ask why?"

Pearl raised her hand.

"Why?" she said. "Why, why, why?"

"Because—of the cameras in the bank parking lot. We get into the van like normal and we drive away. We can't wait there for ten minutes while we stash the money. We have to leave right away, like we would normally do. We drive all the way to New Jersey—it will still be very dark out— and then we pull over for coffee. And while Mom is inside buying us coffee, we slip into the back of the van, we quickly lift up the floor panels, neatly lay out all the money. Then put the floor back. Then we drive away."

"But," Marisol said, "you will wait for me to get back with the coffee—"

"Of course, Mom."

"Will the money fit?" I asked.

"It's all in hundred-dollar bills. Ten hundreds is a thousand. Ten-thousand hundreds is a million. I looked it all up. Now, you get the length, width and thickness of one bill and multiply them together and you get the volume of one bill. Then you multiply that volume by 10,000 and you get the volume of a million dollars if it's all in one stack. Which is 49 inches tall. But we have 39 million dollars so that's 1,911 inches tall. Which is 159 feet."

"Are you sure, my Carlos?"

"Math doesn't lie, Mom."

"We would need a very tall van."

"Yes—if we put it all in one stack—1,911 inches tall. But if we put it in 2 stacks then each would be 955 inches tall. Or we put it in 4 stacks that are each 478 inches tall. Or 8 stacks that are each 239 inches tall. Or 16 stacks that are each 119 inches tall. Or 32 stacks that are each 60 inches tall. Or 64 stacks that are each 30 inches tall. Or 128 stacks that are each 15 inches tall. Or 256 stacks that are about 7 inches tall. Or 512 stacks that are each a little under 4 inches tall. Three-and-a-half inches. That's what we'll do. We lift up the floor of the van and we put down 512 stacks of money. That's 16 columns of money going across and 32 columns going down. Sixteen rows, if you prefer the term rows, with 32 stacks in each row. It will easily fit. We can do it. It will work."

"Good for you, my Carlos. Good for you. Let's go and do it!"

"Damn it, Carlos. You still haven't said how we open the vault!"

"Okay. Listen. At 10:45, the guard leaves. We don't use their computers. It would leave a trail. Instead, I use this laptop. I hack into the website for Falmouth Air and I change the time. I make it 8:55 A.M. on Monday morning. Then I go to the website for the Iron Street branch of Boston United Savings Bank—I hack into their code. And I switch the time source. I change where they get their time from. I change it from the National Institute of Standards—to—Falmouth Air! The bank gets its time from Falmouth Air. See? See what happens? The bank now thinks it's 8:55 A.M. on Monday morning. Well, it would be 8:57 A.M. by then."

"You can hack the site in two minutes?" Todd asked.

"Yep. I've practiced. But even if it takes me five minutes or six minutes or even seven minutes—it's still okay as long as I get it done by what the bank thinks is 9:02 A.M. on Monday morning. Because—because—are you listening Todd—because the bank vault is set to open automatically at 9:03 A.M. on Monday morning."

"How in the world do you know that?" Todd asked.

"He must have used his Google friend," Marisol said.

"No," Carlos responded. "I didn't have to Google it. Remember when I went to the bank to open a safe-deposit box? For all of us?"

"For Dad's watch and Mom's jewelry—" I said.

"Yes. Well, I asked when I could get into the vault, and the teller—you know, the cute blonde with the really short hair? Anyway, she sort of was flirting with me and said, 'Oh, you can get in at 9:03. That's when the vault door opens.'"

I smiled.

"A simple little slip," Carlos said. "From a girl who thought I was cute and wanted to be funny. No Google, no hacking, no bribery. All it took was my winning smile."

"You are so full of yourself," Todd said, laughing.

"Not as full as that vault will be with money," Carlos said. "The vault opens at 9:03. The vault will open because I will make it open. We go in. We take the money. We shut the door. We change the time back on Falmouth Air. We change the code back on the Iron Street branch. The vault is locked and it will remain locked until 9:03 A.M. on Monday morning. The real Monday morning."

Carlos smiled.

"Suppose—" Todd asked, "—suppose you can't do it? Suppose it doesn't work?"

"If I can't open the vault, we finish cleaning the bank and we go home and it's over. No harm, no foul. But—listen to me—it will work."

"I know it will, my Carlos."

"Thanks, Mom."

"You're entirely welcome, my Carlos."

Marisol frowned.

"What is it, Mom?"

"I do not look good in coveralls," Marisol said.

"You look good in anything," Pearl shot out. "And you know it."

"Thank you, Pearl."

"Am I wearing coveralls too?" Pearl asked. "I kind of thought I'd wait in the van."

"No. You can't wait in the van. You'd be noticed. No. We have to take you inside and you have to pretend that you are working with us."

"But—" Pearl started to say.

"We're going to put you in the ladies room to clean the toilets. So all we have to do is get you by the guard and into the ladies room. And you'll stay there until we're finished and ready to make our getaway."

"You will not leave Pearl in the ladies room, like you might leave me in the coffee parking lot will you?"

"No one is going to be left anywhere," Carlos yelled.

"How will Pearl get the money in her coveralls?" Marisol asked.

"Pearl isn't going to have any money in her coveralls," Carlos said. "That way—if we run into some huge problem and we have to get at the money—well—"

"You won't have to deal with a blind girl."

"Exactly. Hope you don't mind."

"Not at all."

"Good. And Mom won't have money in her coveralls either," Carlos added.

"Why not?" Marisol asked.

"Because you're not going inside the vault. You're going to remain outside and keep an eye on things."

"I'm the lookout?"

"Exactly."

"I wanted to be the lookout," Pearl said.

"Pearl!"

"And," Carlos said to Marisol, "if anything happens, you text us."

"So," Marisol said. "Only the boys get the money."

"Exactly. Tim, Todd and me. We go into the vault. We need, as we know, 512 stacks of money. We fit 2 stacks in each pocket. So we need 256 pockets. Now, 256 divided by 3 equals 85. So we each need 85 pockets sewn into the coveralls."

"Wait a minute," Pearl said. "I was just figuring. Eighty-five times 3 is 255. We're a pocket short."

"My coveralls will have 86 pockets sewn in. I get the extra pocket. Don't you think I can divide?"

"Of course," Pearl said, backing down. "Just wanted to—"

"Can 85 pockets fit inside a pair of coveralls?" I asked, trying to divert Carlos from Pearl.

"I took a pair of coveralls," Carlos began, with a bit of strain showing in his voice, "and I taped one-dollar bills to them to simulate the pockets."

"You actually taped money to your coveralls?" Pearl said, smiling. "You mathematicians are all the same."

"But—" Marisol interrupted, "they will be hundred dollar bills, my Carlos."

"All money is the same size, Mom. This is the United States. Not Casablanca."

"Why are you so tense, my Carlos?"

"I'm tense—"

Carlos caught himself.

"It's a lot to get through. I knew that. So, listen. I taped dollar bills—simulating hundred-dollar bills—all over the coveralls. There's plenty of room. We can sew 25 pockets into each leg. That's 50. And the other pockets inside the waist, the back and the front. But my coveralls also needs a pouch for the laptop."

"I see—" Pearl said.

No one laughed.

"So," Carlos went on, "when we get into the parking lot in New Jersey, we don't have to measure anything. Each pocket has 2 stacks."

"And then—?" Pearl asked.

"Then we drive to Belize."

"There's a lot more to this," I said. "There has to be."

"Of course there's a lot more. We have to go to church for instance."

"What?"

"We have to go to the Church of Divine Faith in West Roxbury. We have to go every Sunday and we have to get involved."

"Why in the world—?"

"Because we're telling the world that we are driving to Mexico to do missionary work. We're going to help build a school in Tekoh, Mexico. Which is a hundred miles or so north of the Belize border. This is part of BankJob's program to do good and give back to the world for all of our great success."

"They speak Spanish in Mexico," Marisol said. "I will be very useful."

"Yes. For only for a matter of hours. We're not staying in Tekoh. We're not even driving into Tekoh. We're just using that as a ploy to get by the border guards at the Mexican border. Which we have to do by 9:03 A.M. on Monday morning."

"Can it be done?" I asked.

"I'm sure Carlos figured that out," Todd said.

"Yes. And thank you, Todd. It can be done. We can drive from Boston to the border crossing at Laredo, Texas, which is 2,157 miles, in approximately 32 hours. But by the time we leave the bank, we'll have about 32 hours. So, we can't stop for bathroom breaks."

Carlos smiled broadly.

I hadn't seen him so content—so relaxed—since Linda died. I was so happy for him.

"Wait a minute," Pearl said.

We looked at her.

"Oh," Pearl said, "never mind. It's stupid. It's like dividing 256 by 3. Never mind. I should just be quiet."

"No," Carlos said, "what were you going to say?"

"No. No. Not important at all. Just a thought I thought I had. But I'm sure it's covered. I'm sure it's in one of those circles or squares."

"Don't forget the triangles," Marisol said.

Carlos sighed.

"Look, Pearl. I admit I'm tired. And I admit I carry on. And I admit I got a little ticked off when you asked me—me—a question about long division. I'm sorry. Please. Please just tell me what you were going to ask."

"Well," Pearl began and then stopped.

"Come on, Pearl," Carlos said. "What?"

"Well— What about the cameras inside the bank? How do we not get seen going in and out of the vault?"

Carlos froze.

Carlos didn't say a word.

A look of horror came over his face.

"It can't be done," he said. "I missed that. It can't be done. The plan is no good."

There was another silence.

I thought Carlos would cry. I thought Carlos would collapse.

"Wait a minute," Todd said. "It's only one glitch."

"It's not one glitch," Carlos snapped. "It's the whole plan. I didn't think of the cameras inside the bank. Inside the freaking bank! How could I have missed something that was so obvious? I thought of all the details. Except for the most basic detail of all. What a fool I am!"

"No," Todd said. "Listen. You've figured everything else out. Even the church business. There's got to be a way around the cameras. Come on, Carlos. Let's make some coffee and think this out."

We made a huge pot of coffee.

But Carlos was lost.

We drank hot black caffeine, we talked to Carlos, we said that all of us together should be able to figure this through.

But Carlos was lost.

"Why don't we just spray-paint the camera lenses," Pearl said.

"No," Carlos answered. "That would be seen at the security office and there would be cops there in minutes."

"Can we hack the cameras?" I asked.

"I don't know how," Carlos said. "I could look into it. But if they went off line, police would come right away."

"Why not," Pearl said, "make a big cardboard poster—actual size of the vault entrance. We slide it into place and we sneak in behind it."

"That couldn't work," Carlos said. "They'd see it. They'd see it move. This is so stupid. How could I have not thought of that. I'm so sorry. I'm so sorry."

Carlos put his head down on the table. He raised himself up again and looked at his huge flow chart. Looking for a symbol—a circle, a square or a triangle—that would give him the answer.

A low moan came out of Carlos and he threw his head back down on the table and slowly pounded the tabletop with his fists.

"What a damn fool I am," Carlos hissed. "What a damn fool."

The air left the room.

"I can do it," Marisol said.

Carlos stopped at Marisol's voice. He looked up at her.

"What?" Carlos asked. "What can you do?"

"I can do it. I can do it so that we get in and out without being seen. I know how to do it."

Carlos looked at his mother. A thin hint of a smile came across his face.

"In the security office, where they watch the TVs," Marisol said, "how many men are there?"

"Two," Carlos answered.

"Both of them are men?"

"Yes. I checked it out."

"And when we go into the vault, how long will they have been working?"

"About six hours. They work eight-hour shifts. So—yes—they'd have been working for six hours."

"Can you three boys get into the vault and get the money and get out—in ten minutes?"

"We can do it in six minutes. At most eight minutes."

"Then I know how to do it."

"How?"

"Oh. I know the way."

CHAPTER TWENTY-THREE
You Gotta Have Faith

We liked church.

The Reverend Phillippe DuValle welcomed us with enthusiasm. The Church of Divine Faith was a raucous event. Lots of singing. Lots of personal testimonials. And the Reverend's sermon was all about paying back. Giving back.

This was right up our alley.

After the service, we went downstairs for the coffee-and-pastry reception.

We decided to let Marisol do the talking.

"Father Reverend," she said, belying her nominally Catholic upbringing, "all of us have had a lot in this life and then we lost most of it—and now we have some of it back. And—like you say today—we want to do right and give back to the world."

This sort of conversation went on for six weeks.

We went to church on Sundays. Well, at least two of us went on Sunday. We figured that if we all went, it might come across as a little too much. So we played it close to the vest.

Marisol went every week. She dressed to kill—in a demure church sort of way. She stood when the congregation stood. She belted out hymns. She raised her hand to Heaven once. Only once. But it was effective.

Eventually Marisol and Phillippe—they were on a first-name basis by then—came to an accord.

"Reverend Father Phillippe," Marisol had said, "I was telling my boys recently that I would like to be a teacher."

"That's a wonderful vocation," he replied.

"Well, I think it's hard work. It's not sitting in the sun."

The Reverend let that go.

"Why do you want to teach?" he said.

"I love the children. I love talking to children. I have—a lot to say."

"Then you should teach, my dear," he said.

"But I have not gone to college. I don't have the degrees. I have never taught. But I know—in my heart—that I would be a good teacher."

The Reverend had an affiliation with a church in Campeche—not Tekoh, as Carlos has planned.

"Who cares?" Carlos said. "Tell him we're in. Get him to write letters. Tell him we have to leave on May 17, because of our work schedule. That should give him plenty of time to get our visas in order."

That's exactly what happened.

On the first of May, we had visas to go to Mexico for missionary work. We had letters of introduction. We had three cases of Bibles and three more cases of *Dick and Jane* readers. Our mission—so to speak—was to go to Campeche, hook up with the pastor, and spend three weeks in their elementary school—teaching the kids to read English and then to read the Bible.

"I will feel so terrible when we never go," Marisol said to all of us over dinner that night. "I wanted to be a teacher. We are going to let them down. And the Father Reverend Phillippe has been so nice to us. With the singing and the coffee and the pastry. I feel like I've lied to him."

"You did lie to him," Carlos said.

"Carlos! I did not tell the lie."

"Are we going to Campeche?" Carlos asked. "Are we going to teach children to read?"

"No we are not. But it was not a lie in my heart! I wanted to teach the children! I wanted them to meet Dick and Jane."

"We'll send them a hundred thousand dollars," Carlos said. "Once we are in Belize, we'll send the church a hundred thousand dollars."

"Fine," Marisol said. "That's the best we can do, I suppose."

"Why don't we teach in Belize?" Pearl shot out.

"What do you mean?" I asked.

"Well—think about it. What are we going to do there? All this planning has been to rob the money and make our getaway. But once we are got away—you know—what are we going to do with our lives there?"

That was a very good question indeed.

"Pearl," Marisol said, "I always like the way you think your thoughts. Especially right now. Tim, Todd, Carlos. I want to be a teacher. In Belize, we don't have to worry about degrees and licenses, right?"

"Of course not," I said. "We can simply start a school if we want. They have public schools, of course, but who's to stop us from opening a private school? It can be after school if we run into objections. Like a special school. Or on weekends. Or during the summer."

"What will we teach?" Marisol asked.

"Well," Carlos replied, "They speak English. But there are lots of ethnic groups in Belize. Mayan and Mestizo and Kriol. They might need help with English. And then we could teach Spanish—well, Mom can."

"I can teach braille," Pearl said.

There was a pause.

"That's not a joke," she said. "There have to be blind kids there, right? I can teach them braille."

"And," Todd threw out, "we can teach math. Lord knows we can teach math."

"That takes care of the school," I said. "Now, what about the hospital?"

"What do you mean?" Todd asked.

"If I'm going to Belize, I'm going to practice medicine."

"I wish I could be your nurse," Pearl said.

"We'll see," I answered. "We'll see."

Things were taking shape.

"We need land," Carlos said. "Land there is pretty cheap. We'll need a lot of acres; and there has to be a big villa for all of us. And then there has to be some outbuildings that we can use for the school and the hospital."

"Let's look right now!" Pearl screamed.

We were on our way. Carlos throw open his laptop and did a quick search.

"Look!" he yelled. "This is amazing! Look at this one. Four hundred and forty acres. Roads. Its own pond. A large house. Look at that house! Two verandas. First- and second-floor verandas!"

"I love a good veranda!" Todd yelled. "There's nothing, I would imagine, like smoking cigars on a veranda overlooking the Caribbean Sea."

"You don't smoke cigars," Marisol said.

"I'm going to start. I'm going to smoke the big ones."

"Churchills," I said. "I smoked Churchills in medical school. It was a fad. And—we can buy Cubans in Belize."

"You mean slaves?" Marisol said.

"No. Not slaves. Cuban cigars. Cohibas. Castro's cigars. Politics aside, the man knows his cigars."

"Look at the floor plan," Carlos yelled. "There are rooms everywhere. There are twelve bedrooms on the second floor. Each with its own bath. And each with French doors that open onto the veranda—that looks out at the Caribbean. And there are open-air spaces. And patios. And look at this kitchen, Mom. It's huge!"

"What does it cost, Carlos?"

"Oh. Let's see. Oh, here it is. Nine hundred thousand dollars."

"We can afford that," Marisol said. "My teacher's salary will pay for it."

CHAPTER TWENTY-FOUR
Wrinkle Cream

May 16 was a very warm and sunny day.

I was usually the first one up. I'd turn on the coffee and read the paper while the coffee perked—and then I'd bring up a tray and two cups of coffee for Pearl and me. We'd sit in bed and let the caffeine soak into our bloodstream and talk of this and that and maybe a little more of that.

But on May 16, Todd raced into the kitchen.

"What's up?" I asked.

"I have a few wrinkles."

"You're getting old? If you're getting old, then I'm getting old. Get it? We're twins."

"I have a couple of ideas that I think will make things a lot better."

"What are they?"

"I'm not sure you'll think it's a good idea. Let's talk on the way."

"On the way to where?" I asked.

"Augie's. We have to go see Augie."

I ran upstairs with the coffee tray.

"Sorry, Pearl, I can't sit and talk today. I've got to run out with Todd."

"Give me the coffee—"

I handed her a cup and left the carafe on the bedside table and ran down and then out with Todd.

Augie, our service-station man, said he could help. When we explained why, he said he didn't want to be paid. It would be his contribution to the good work of the church.

I was starting to protest, when Todd gave me the eye.

As we drove home, Todd said, "It's good that he bought in so deeply. If questioned—there will be no doubt in his mind."

"You think he'll be questioned by the police?" I asked.

"I think everyone we've ever met will be questioned by the police."

"Wow. Think if they go to Headmaster Winn. Or our professors at Harvard."

"Of course they'll question them."

"You're right—it's good that Augie believes in supporting the work of the Lord."

During the next four hours, we drove all the way to Leominster in western Massachusetts and parked the car a few blocks away from a sign store. We went inside and bought four pieces of white, magnetic vinyl, with each piece measuring two feet by two feet.

On the way home, following directions that Todd had worked out on his iPhone, we repeated the process at two more sign stores in two different towns.

"Okay," Todd said. "That's six feet across by four feet high. For each side. That will do it. It's possible that some really brilliant cop could trace the purchases we just made—but the statistical probability of that is negligible. And—as with the the rest of these wrinkles—if they ever were to figure it out, well, we're no worse off."

We drove home and went inside and talked with the gang. I was thinking of us as a gang. I wanted a good name. The best I could do was, The Hole in the Vault Gang. No one liked it. Not even me.

At any rate, Todd told our nameless gang that we needed to use both vans.

"What do you mean we need both vans?" Carlos asked.

"Todd has a couple of wrinkles," I said.

"I have none of the wrinkles," Marisol said. "It is not because I use the expensive creams. It is because I come from good blood. Even the men in our family get no wrinkles."

Todd explained the wrinkles—his brand of wrinkles—to Carlos, Marisol and Pearl.

"Well," Pearl said, "that does add a layer of risk. But—if it all works—"

"We're much better off if it all works," Todd said. "And if it doesn't, we're only out a little money. Well. Two hundred thousand dollars is not a little money. But when you compare it to approximately thirty-nine million dollars, it does tend to get lost."

That was it.

Todd and I picked up the van at 6:00 P.M. Augie had done a great job. The van now had a pristine coat of new white paint. And in the center of the side panels on both sides was painted a small but readable logo. Two small hands clasped as if in prayer. And underneath the hands, in small red letters: Church of Divine Faith.

We drove it home and parked it next to the other BankJob van which Carlos had gotten an hour before. It wasn't common—but certainly not unusual—for us to drive the vans home for the night. Our neighbors wouldn't think it strange.

Before bed, each of us packed one knapsack of clothes and essentials. We took them out and loaded them in the back of the "church" van.

Then we congregated for chocolate and cognac in the living room.

"Here is to us all of us," Marisol said.

"To us," we echoed.

"And to Martinez," Carlos said.

"And to Mom," I said.

"And to Dad," Todd said.

"And to my sister," Pearl said.

"This," Marisol said, "is so happy and so sad."

There was nothing to add. We finished our cognac and chocolate. We went to bed.

CHAPTER TWENTY-FIVE
BankJob

I remember nothing of the morning, afternoon or early evening of May 17.

But from ten o'clock on, the human video of what transpired is printed indelibly in my mind.

At exactly 10:00 P.M., we drove both vans into the parking lot behind the bank and parked them side-by-side in front of the loading dock.

The "church" van—the van with the fake floor boards—had its logo covered on either side by the magnetic vinyl sheets we had bought. To each of these was taped sheets of paper that Todd had printed. It was like a jigsaw puzzle. A composite. When put together, they replicated the BankJob logo and covered up the church logo.

We got out of the vans. We were already in our coveralls—well, everyone except Marisol. She carried hers.

Carlos did a lot of sham pointing for the benefit of the cameras—as if he were explaining the ropes to newbies.

We went inside.

The security guard wouldn't be there until 10:30, but we got to work right away.

Pearl and I had rehearsed walking side-by-side that morning; the idea being to get her from the back door and into the ladies' room without doing anything to attract attention from the all-seeing lenses.

"You're doing great," I said. "If I were watching, I'd think you could see."

"I'm so nervous," she said. "My heart is skipping. Stay close."

"I am. And—we're about to turn—now."

I pushed open the door and Pearl went before me. We were inside. I guided her to the first stall and showed her where to kneel down and handed her a scrub brush.

"You have to swish the brush around when the guard is here," I said. "But he won't go inside the ladies' room."

"I got it," she answered.

I was getting up to leave, when she grabbed my arm and impulsively kissed me.

"I love my bandit," she said.

"You're a bandit too," I replied.

"Go crack the safe and don't forget me when it's over," she said and knelt down again, her brush at the ready.

I went back out into the bank's main area. Carlos did some more sham pointing and barked some sham orders and we split up and got to work.

The guard walked in at 10:35.

"I'm running five minutes behind," he said to Carlos as he moved to the time clock to punch in.

Then he stopped and looked at us, spread out around the bank.

"Where are the Alonzos?" he asked.

"They weren't scheduled tonight," Carlos said. "This is one of our bonus cleanups. And we figured we'd break in our two new employees. Because—

He lowered his voice to a whisper.

"If they—you know—screw up—the bank won't even notice. They probably will screw up. But—it's good practice for them."

"Why two vans?" the guard asked.

"We wanted both of them them to drive. To get used to it. Eventually, they'll be going to different banks. So, I wanted them to get some experience."

"Never easy, is it," the guard said.

"Well, good help is hard to find."

With that, the guard walked around a bit—looked into offices—gave the vault door a reassuring pat and then nodded to Marisol.

"Hello, there," he said.

"Hello," Marisol said. "You are the bank guard? That is a big job."

"Why aren't you dressed?" he asked.

The three of us froze.

"Oh," Marisol said, "I do not look so good in coveralls. So I put them on when I get here."

Then she leaned in and whispered to the guard, "I really don't like to wear them outside—you know—where—men can see me."

140

She smiled at him and he nodded again.

With that the guard left and went off on his next set of appointed rounds.

We were alone in the bank.

Todd, Carlos, Pearl, Marisol and me.

We looked to Carlos for direction.

"I need five minutes," he said.

He went into the men's room—where, as with the ladies' room, there are no security cameras—and took his laptop out from under his coveralls and sat on the floor and turned it on.

He locked onto the WiFi and in another thirty seconds he was looking at the site for Falmouth Air.

Marisol took this opportunity to step into the ladies' room.

"Pearl, the guard is gone and Carlos is in the men's room with his computer."

"Okay. Thanks."

"I have to get to work," Marisol said.

"Okay. Good luck. Don't forget me when it's over."

"You? No one could ever forget you, Pearl."

Marisol came out and joined us. She picked up her pair of coveralls and held them up before her as if she were inspecting a gown by Ralph Lauren.

Carlos came out of the men's room—zipping up his fly for benefit of the cameras—and started pointing around as if he were giving instructions as to what had to be cleaned.

"We're doing well," he said. "Time to empty the trash cans."

That was the signal.

Todd and I started going from desk to desk picking up trash cans and emptying them into a large rubber bin on wheels. Carlos busied himself straightening all the chairs around the office.

Meanwhile, at the control desk of HTSB—High Tech Security of Boston—Bill and Jake, longtime employees who had spent way too many hours watching nothing happen on TV screens pointed all over the city, were sitting at a long curved counter that held fourteen video monitors.

I had no way of knowing this of course, but, if Marisol was right about men—and who could ever be more right about men than La Marisol—then Bill and Jake would behave in a manner that Marisol anticipated. If she were wrong about men—then this little vision of mine would turn out to be a total fantasy and I would be behind bars somewhere dark and dank—regretting that I had ever let Marisol talk us into this predicament. We let her talk us into this because we believed in Marisol. We believed in Marisol because she believed in herself.

At HTSB, Bill was checking out the monitors to the left. Jake was concentrating on the monitors to the right.

Jake's eye was caught by the monitor that was hooked up to the nine cameras at the Iron Street branch of Boston United Savings Bank.

Three rows of three images filled the screen.

Jake gave the little video boxes a cursory glance. He saw Todd in one box. He saw me in another. And he saw Carlos in a third. Then he noticed the video box in the upper-right-hand corner.

"Bill. Bill—"

"What?"

"Look at this—"

Bill turned his glaze toward Jake.

"Bill. Look at this monitor. It's—it's Iron Street. Look up there. To the right."

"It's a woman."

"It's a woman taking her clothes off!"

Bill stood and walked over to get a better look.

"You're right."

"Of course I'm right."

Bill took the mouse out of Jake's hand and clicked it.

The image in the upper-right-hand corner now filled the entire screen. The views from the other eight cameras were not visible for the moment.

Marisol was sitting on the edge of a desk, leaning back a bit, wistfully unbuttoning her blouse. It was a red blouse. A very bright red blouse. Marisol zipped through the buttons and the blouse opened wide, revealing her full breasts straining against a bra of jet-black lace.

"Look at her!" Bill said.

Marisol dropped the blouse down onto the desk top.

Then she stood and shook her head to swish her hair back and forth.

"Wow!" Jake said.

Marisol slowly—very, very slowly—slid off her white skirt, and slipped it off of her heels and tossed that onto the desk as well.

"Look at her. Is that—?"

"A garter belt. I've seen them in Victoria's Secret—"

"Victoria's Secret? At the mall?"

"No. Online."

"Oh."

Marisol was by herself in a corner, out of sight of Todd, Carlos and me.

The three of us still had no way of knowing what Bill and Jake were doing. All we knew was that if there was going to be a moment—well, that moment was at hand.

I took one deep breath and walked toward the vault. Todd and Carlos got there as well. Carlos reached up and put his hand on the silver wheel that was the door latch. If we were being watched—well, that didn't affect what we would do next. We'd have no way of knowing if we were being watched. The only signal we'd get would be flashing lights and running footsteps.

If that happened, our plan was to put our hands up and surrender. We'd call our lawyer. And then we'd call the *Boston Globe* and throw ourselves on the mercy of the court of public opinion.

All this was racing through my brain as my eyes riveted themselves on the silver wheel.

Lefty loosey, righty tighty.

That's what I was thinking.

Carlos grabbed the wheel and attempted to give it a left turn.

For the next two minutes—maybe it was three minutes—Marisol used her perfectly manicured fingers, adorned with cobalt-blue nail polish that practically glowed like embers on the computer monitor, to slowly, very slowly, unbutton one black fishnet nylon stocking. When the fasteners were undone she started to slowly, oh so slowly, roll down her stocking. Pausing now and again to sort of casually look around the room and lick her dark-red lips.

Todd, Carlos and I—naturally—saw none of Marisol's performance.

Todd, Carlos and I were in the vault staring at three bins of money. They looked like laundry bins that you see in hotels—not too big, dirty canvas, rectangular—totally unassuming.

Except that each one held thirteen million dollars.

"Thirty-nine million dollars," I said.

"Approximately," Carlos replied.

Much faster than Marisol, we were out of our coveralls. Each of us knelt before a bin and methodically took out the stacks of hundred-dollar bills, each wrapped by a paper band, and we put them in pockets inside the coveralls.

Out in the bank, Marisol turned her attention to the second stocking. To ensure her audience didn't wander, she stood up and with her back to the camera she bent over and started to lower her remaining black-lace fishnet wonder.

Inside the vault we were almost done.

Our plan was not to speak. We didn't think there was any sound recording going on, but we weren't going to take a chance.

Carlos motioned with his eyes that we should hurry.

"Why can't my wife wear that kind of stuff?" Jake said, putting his face nearly up to the surface of the monitor.

"Because she gave up trying a long time ago. Just like my wife."

"How come *she* hasn't given up?" Jake asked, pointing at Marisol on the screen.

"Maybe—"

Bill caught himself.

"How long have we been watching her?" he asked.

"I don't know," Jake said. "Three minutes."

Bill looked at the monitor.

"Seven minutes," he said. "Look at the timer. It's been seven minutes."

Jake nodded.

"Why is she doing this? Now? Today?"

"She's changing for work," Jake said. "She's over in the corner because she didn't want the others to see."

"Why didn't she go into the ladies' room to change?" Bill asked.

"Girls don't like changing in bathrooms. Besides, the other girl is in there. I saw the other girl go in."

Inside the vault, Carlos motioned with his eyes that we had to leave. We had our coveralls back on. He jerked his head toward the vault door a couple of times.

"Look," Jake said, "she's going to put on her coveralls."

"Switch back to the grid view," Bill said. "Let's see what's going on."

Carlos reached out and grabbed each of us with an outstretched hand. We started toward the vault door. I slipped free from him. I was struggling with my zipper. I couldn't get it any higher than my waist. It was stuck. Money was visible. I couldn't be seen like this!

"Go to the full-grid view now!" Bill said, his voice rising.

"What's with you?" Jake asked. "Look at her."

In a grand flourish, Marisol stepped into her coveralls and was slowly rolling them up her body. The suit was unfolding upward. It was above her waist and her hands grazed against her breasts as she pulled up the fabric.

"Go to the full grid now!" Bill barked.

Jake clicked the mouse.

All nine images came into view. In the center image in the center row, Bill saw the vault door. It was closed.

In the upper-left video box he saw Carlos straightening a chair up against a desk. In the video box below that, he saw Todd grabbing another trash basket to empty. And in the box below that, he saw me, with my back to the camera, pretending to be bending over to pick up a trash basket.

I pulled on the zipper and this time it shot up.

I grabbed the basket and stood up and dumped the papers into the large trash container.

In the upper right-hand corner of the grid, Marisol zipped up her coveralls and licked her lips one more time and walked over to where we were and said, "I am now ready to work."

"See," Jake said, "everything is normal. Why the panic?"

"Forget it," Bill said. "Keep an eye on them. But—mostly—keep an eye on her."

We cleaned the bank very well if I say so myself. It was a little difficult, walking around in our bulky suits, but we managed.

Marisol went into the ladies room.

"Pearl—"

"Did we do it?"

147

"We did it, Pearl. I told you it would work! And I was right."

"Did you— Did you have to take your clothes off?"

"Not everything. No different than going to the beach. In Belize."

"Good for you, Marisol."

"Thank you, my Pearl."

"Oh—"

"What is it?"

"You called me 'my Pearl.' You've never done that before."

Marisol smiled, even though she knew her smile wouldn't be seen, and then she walked outside to the main area and started her job of straightening all those little transaction slips in the slots under the glass top of the desks with the pens that never had any ink.

On the other side of the main area, Carlos walked over to me and spoke without showing his face to the cameras.

"I didn't realize the coveralls would be this bulky," he said.

"It's okay. We can get our work done."

"I don't care about that," Carlos said. "What about when the guard comes back?"

That would be a problem.

Was there no end to wrinkles?

We heard a car pull up outside the bank.

"It's him," Carlos said. "He's early!"

"You have to change," I said. "Change with Pearl."

"Will the coveralls fit?"

"Pearl is five-seven," I said. "Yours will be a little loose on her, and hers will be a little tight on you. It will work. We have no other choice."

So Carlos ducked into the ladies room and walked up to Pearl and said, "Take off your coveralls. We have to change clothes. Please."

In a flash he and Pearl switched coveralls.

"How much is in this?" Pearl asked.

"Thirteen million dollars."

"Approximately?"

"That's right."

Carlos put on Pearl's coveralls.

"Pearl. Reach inside the coveralls and take out the laptop out of the pouch."

Pearl did a bit of a gyration and extracted the computer. Carlos sat on the floor and opened it up and went right to the site of Falmouth Air and changed the time back to what it should have been. Then he went to the bank site and switched the clock from Falmouth Air back to the National Institute of Standards.

He handed the laptop back to Pearl, and she slipped it inside her coveralls and zipped up.

"Thanks, Pearl," Carlos said. "Now the trains won't crash."

Carlos walked out of the ladies' room and he bumped into the security guard. They were both startled.

"Oh, sorry," Carlos said to the guard. "Can you imagine, that new girl we hired is still cleaning the toilets in the ladies' room? There are only three toilets! Two sinks! I had to go in there and give her a piece of my mind. I don't know if she's going to work out. I only hired her because she really needs a job. She's got two kids."

"Well," the guard said, "give her another chance. She may straighten out."

"Maybe you're right," Carlos said. "I'll give her the benefit of the doubt."

Todd and I were on the other side of the main banking room—so the guard wouldn't get a close look at our coveralls.

I looked as the guard walked away from Carlos, right up to the vault. He put his hand up to the wheel which opened the door.

He was going to try and open the vault.

I looked at Todd with panic. Todd didn't notice me. He was staring at the vault door.

Carlos had a look of benign resignation.

The guard put his hand on the wheel.

He gave the wheel a twist.

Nothing happened.

He gave it another twist.

Nothing happened.

"I do that so they'll know I checked," he said to Carlos, nodding at the cameras, "but I always hope that one night it's going to open and I'll grab a quick million and head to Canada."

Carlos laughed.

"Canada? Not Mexico?"

"Canada is a lot closer."

"Oh. You're right. Never thought of it."

"You guys done?" the guard asked.

"Just finishing. As soon as the new girl takes care of the last toilet—we're done."

"Well—it's nice you're giving her a second chance."

"Yeah. You were right. It's the decent thing to do."

"Okay. I'm off on my next set of rounds. Hey—Sox-Yankees for four games starting on Monday."

"Can't wait," Carlos said.

"Damn Yankees," the guard said.

"Tell me about it."

The guard sort of saluted Carlos in an off-handed way and then he walked out of the bank.

We all froze where we were.

The plan was not to move for five minutes.

Comeback time.

Wait five minutes just in case the guard comes back in.

Carlos would tell us when.

We couldn't freeze completely of course, because of the cameras. So we sort of puttered around—moving things a bit and making things look perfect.

"Time to head out," Carlos shouted. "Tim—don't forget to tell the new girl we're leaving."

I didn't forget.

CHAPTER TWENTY-SIX
Laredo

Todd and I were in the van that had the fake logo on top of the church logo. It also had the fake floor with the fake screws designed to look old and conceal the all-important seam—an image that Carlos had fashioned and honed and sculpted like a Michelangelo masterpiece.

I was driving the masterpiece.

Carlos, Marisol and Pearl were in the unaltered BankJob van. Carlos was driving that van. The three of them were wearing white cotton gloves. A little wrinkle Pearl had thought of only that morning.

We let Carlos lead the way, since we were going to pull in behind him and then back out when we were done.

We drove all the way to the town of Carlisle, to 308 Hancock Street.

It was a giant stone house—with a mansard roof and a huge front entrance.

Carlos pulled into the driveway; it was on the left side of the house, far away from the bedrooms. We knew that because Carlos had looked up the architect online and saw the floor plans.

I sat at the wheel of our van and watched. Todd did the same from the passenger seat.

Carlos, Marisol and Pearl got out of their van.

While driving to this house, Marisol had reached inside Pearl's coveralls and taken out two hundred thousand dollars. She divided it equally and put a hundred thousand in each of two manila envelopes, each of which was labeled with a name. The name was spelled out with letters clipped from the *Boston Globe*—like in ransom notes. Except this was sort of a reverse ransom.

She handed the envelopes to Carlos when they got out.

Marisol and Pearl clambered into the back row of seats in our van, while Carlos opened the back door of the BankJob van. He got inside quickly, carrying the two manila envelopes, and he put them in a tool case.

Then Carlos got out and shut the back doors and locked the van up tight. He leaned over and placed the keys on the inside bottom lip of the rear bumper. Carlos walked around our van and took off the magnetic sheets that covered the BankJob logo—revealing to all the world that we were driving a van belonging, at least in terms of intent, to the Church of Divine Faith. But all the world didn't see him, because there were no security cameras in Crummy Pig's driveway.

Then Carlos got into the back row of our van, slipped the magnetic sheets under the seat, and sat with Marisol and Pearl. I backed out of the driveway and we were off. The stop had taken less than three minutes.

No one said a word for a while.

I drove quickly—but at the speed limit.

When we got onto the MassPike heading west, I could feel the tension melt away.

"What exit?" Todd asked.

"Exit 9," I said. "Interstate 84—South. Then Interstate 91 South. I have the route memorized. Didn't want to chance printing it or even putting it into a GPS."

"Then what?" Todd asked.

"Then 287 West. Then 78 West. Then 81 South. Then—let's see—then 40—then 75—then 24—then 59—then 12—then 10—then 69. Those are all interstates. Then it's U.S. State Route 59."

"And then?" Todd asked.

"Then—yipee-ki-ay—we're in Laredo."

"I like the sound of Laredo," Marisol said.

"So do I," I said. "But remember—we have to find a mailbox on the American side before we cross into Mexico."

Then we were silent.

The miles dissolved before us. The van was in fine tune and the road was straight and clear.

Three hundred miles later we were in New Jersey.

I pulled into a rest area right on Interstate 287—we didn't want to get off the highway.

It was three in the morning. Still plenty dark.

Marisol slid out of her coveralls—with a lot less fanfare this time—and then she went into the restaurant to buy five coffees. Todd and I climbed into the back seat to join Carlos and Pearl. The seat was the only divider from the rear of the van. It was one big open space.

So Carlos simply climbed over the back seat to get into the back of the van. Down on his hands and knees, he felt under the back seat with his hand—searching for a very small black button attached to the underside of the seat. He found it. He switched off the magnets. It was easy to lift up the right side of the floor. He leaned the sheet up against the side of the van.

Meanwhile, Pearl took off her coveralls and then handed them to Carlos, who quickly took out the stacks of money and laid them down in rows. When done, he put Pearl's coveralls and his own coveralls on top of the money. He placed the laptop down. He tossed in the cotton gloves. Pearl threw him Marisol's coveralls and they went in as well. Then, on top of the coveralls, he put the twelve magnetic sheets with the BankJob paper logo.

Carlos climbed over the back seat and his place was taken by me.

I did the same thing with the money and the coveralls.

Then it was Todd's turn.

By then we were on the left side of the van.

Todd finished putting his money and coveralls down—and then quickly got back over the seat with us.

And there it was. Thirty-nine million dollars. Approximately. Plus all the evidence of what we had done.

Carlos climbed back and carefully lined up the two sides of the fake floor. When it met his satisfaction, he reached under the seat and pushed the little black button again.

"It's locked and loaded," he said with a hint of a smile. "Get it? Locked? Loaded?"

We got it.

Marisol returned with coffee. Five identical cups of black coffee. She handed them out and everyone got back in their original seats.

Our gang lacked a name—but did not suffer from a lack of mathematical exactness.

I drove to the pumps and filled the van with gas. I paid with cash. No credit-card trail.

We were back on the interstate.

"Keep an eye out for Route 78," I said to Todd. "That's our next step."

Taking turns driving and sleeping, we moved south and west, inexorably toward Laredo.

At 9:00 A.M. on Sunday morning, Todd was driving and I was sleeping.

I came awake to Pearl's voice.

"No news yet."

She was reading the news on the internet—actually listening to the news on the internet with a special electronic reader she had.

"Nothing yet. I'm looking at Boston.com, NewYorkTimes.com and CNN.com. Nothing. Nothing about a bank. Nothing about the van we left."

"Do you have to say 'looking'?" Marisol asked.

"All right. I'm listening to those sites."

"Did you check the police logs?" Carlos asked. "Remember I showed you how."

"Yep. Nothing. I'm surprised there's nothing about the van."

"There won't be," Carlos said, "until after 11:00 A.M .on Monday morning. At the earliest."

"Why?" Pearl asked.

"Because that's when Crummy Pig gets back from vacation. His flight lands at Logan at nine. So—figure an hour or so to get a cab and get home. Then he sees this van in his driveway. It's locked. He has no choice but to call the police."

"That's two hours after the bank vault opens," Marisol said. "But, my Carlos—suppose Crummy Pig panics and doesn't call the police?"

"He'll have no idea what the van is all about," Carlos answered.

"But that's another wrinkle," Todd said.

"What is this wrinkle?" Marisol asked.

"I bought a prepaid cellphone," Todd said, "which is on and fully charged—and I put it in the lower-right-hand drawer of the desk of Mario Mollacare."

"The manager of the bank we just robbed?" Marisol asked. "Who used to be the big shoot at the bank?"

"Big shot," Carlos said.

"Yes," Todd continued. "I programmed the phone to send a text message to the police station in Carlisle. It's set to be delivered at 10:30 A.M. on Monday morning. Reporting a mysterious van parked in the ever-so-exclusive Carlisle neighborhood. The police may even beat Crummy Pig to the house."

"Look," I said. "We're entering Tennessee."

None of us had ever been to Tennessee.

Against Carlos' wishes, we stopped for breakfast. We actually pulled off the highway—off of the interstate—and stopped at a small diner called Angela's.

"I like the name Angela," Marisol said. "It's like the angels."

"This is a big mistake," Carlos said. "We're wasting time. We'll be seen."

"Who's going to remember us?" I said.

"Oh, yeah. You're right. A set of twins. An Hispanic man. His mother who takes her clothes off in public. And—oh—let us not forget the blind girl. What's there to remember?"

"At least we are not wearing the coveralls," Marisol said.

"At least you're wearing something," Carlos replied.

"We have to eat," Marisol said. "I want to sit and eat. I want a big hot breakfast. And then you can drive straight to Laredo and I will complain no more."

Pearl put on sunglasses and I held hands with her—like we were on a date—and we walked in and sat at the first booth we found with no one noticing she was blind.

The waitress came over and before she could ask us what we wanted, Carlos said, "Hi. We'll all have that breakfast special on the board there. And five black coffees. Thanks."

"Where you all from?" she asked.

"Boston," Carlos said. "Heading home in fact."

She smiled and walked away.

"She's in the back room, calling the cops. Tennessee cops. Who sleep with shotguns."

"She's not calling the cops," I said. "Let's just eat and hit the road."

"No one speak to anyone," he said.

"May we speak to each other, Carlos?" Marisol asked.

He gave her a look.

"Carlos. My Carlos. I took off my clothes to distract the guards. That was the wrinkle we talked about."

"That wasn't the wrinkle," Carlos said. "That wasn't the wrinkle at all. The wrinkle was leaving the van in the driveway of Shel Crummins' mansion in Carlisle. The wrinkle was leaving two manilla envelopes with a hundred thousand dollars in each one—addressed to Clive Williams and Jonathan Slocum. The wrinkle was leaving the cellphone in the desk of Mario Mollacare. The next wrinkle will be mailing the letter giving our entire business—all of it—to Juanita Alonzo. The final wrinkle will be mailing the letter giving Marisol's house to the Church of Divine Faith. Those are the wrinkles."

"This is another very good wrinkle," Marisol said. "Eating here is a good wrinkle."

"It's not another wrinkle," Carlos whispered. "The wrinkle is the money that we left that will make the cops spend a heck of a lot of time looking at the executives of United Savings Bank of Boston. They can't ignore the money. They can't ignore the paper bands. They can't ignore the connections. If they're good at their jobs—maybe they'll figure out the connections about Shel Crummins stealing all of our money. About how those three guys were involved—but never charged and never punished. Except for poor Mario who was demoted. I'm hoping he'll crack and spill the beans. But if he doesn't and it gets out that the phone message to the police came from his desk, then maybe one of the other three jokers will crack and say something that will implicate them in the fraud—in the swindle. Then—on top of all that—the Alonzos show

159

up with our notarized letter giving them our business—but one of their trucks was involved in the robbery. And the other truck is missing. And just how many Alonzos are there anyway? And are they all accounted for? So what does all that mean? Who knows? Maybe the police will figure something out. Maybe they won't. But at least it's got to distract them for a while. So. *That* was the wrinkle."

"You knew I was going to change my clothes in front of the cameras," Marisol said. "It was nothing, my Carlos. None of us saw it. Only those two guards at the security place."

"I didn't see anything, that's for sure," Pearl said.

"Pearl—"

"They probably taped it," Carlos said.

"Maybe I will be a star on the internet," Marisol said.

"And that will be a big help to us, won't it? They won't figure out that you were distracting them?"

"Wait a minute," Todd said. "Wait a lousy minute. They can't do anything with the tape"

"What are you talking about?" I asked.

"Think of it," Todd said. "It would cost them their jobs. It would prove they were derelict in their duty. They're going to erase the tape. That's what they're going to do."

Carlos nodded his head a couple of times.

"You're right. You're absolutely right. We're in the clear."

Carlos actually smiled.

"So—again I say—my wrinkle was a good thing."

Carlos was going to snap at her, but the waitress arrived with five plates of food and we dug into breakfast.

Twenty-two minutes later we were on the road and on Interstate 40—which was going to be as close to Knoxville as we were ever going to get.

The miles and roads fell before us.

Except when she slept, Pearl monitored the internet for news.

There was no news.

At 2:00 P.M. on Sunday afternoon we had put Chattanooga, Birmingham and Nashville behind us. We had been on 40, 75, 24 and 59.

At 9:00 P.M. we waved at New Orleans.

At midnight, we switched from Interstate 12 to Interstate 10.

"Cowboys and cowgirls," I said, "it's officially Monday. And we are in Texas."

I loved Texas. Well, what I saw of it from the van. It is one big state.

We kept on and on and on.

I pulled over to buy gas and Marisol spotted a mailbox.

"There is the box for the United States mail," she said.

In a flash she was out of the car and striding in her spike heels to the box. She carried a large U.S. Post Office Priority Mail Express prepaid envelope—guaranteed to be delivered the next day—that was addressed to Claire—in care of the Marriott Toronto, where Claire was attending yet another trade show.

In the large mailing envelope were two letters—one to Juanita Alonzo and the other to Phillippe DuValle.

There also was a note on which Pearl had written:

Dear Claire,
Please do me a huge favor and mail these two letters today from a post office in Toronto. With Canadian stamps. And—make sure you rip this note and our mailing envelope to shreds and dispose of the shreds in different trash baskets outside of the hotel.
Don't call me. I'll call you in three days.
Thanks, you ugly witch.
~Pearl

Marisol popped the large envelope into the mailbox, pulled the lid back down to check, and then checked again and then she was back in the van.

"Those postmarks," Todd said, "should point the police toward our neighbors to the north."

We kept driving.

No one wanted to stop for anything.

We kept on and on and on.

At exactly 8:45 A.M., Eastern Standard Time—6:45 A.M. in Texas—we drove up to the border-crossing station in Laredo. We could see Mexico.

"The vault," Carlos said, "will open in 18 minutes."

CHAPTER TWENTY-SEVEN
When Eyes Can See

I was driving. Pearl was in the front passenger seat.

In the seat behind us, Carlos sat on the driver's side, Marisol was in the middle and Todd was on the passenger side.

I stopped the van and put down the window and smiled at the border-patrol guard.

"Good morning," he said.

"Good morning," I answered.

"Documents—"

I handed him our passports—open and stacked inside each other. I handed him our visas.

"Purpose for going to Mexico?"

"We are doing missionary work. For the Church of Divine Faith in Massachusetts. We have bibles and reading textbooks with us and we're going to Campeche. To the Church of Our Lady of Lourdes. We're going to work there for three weeks."

"Everything seems in order," he said.

I nodded.

"Shut the motor off."

"Excuse me?"

"Shut the motor off."

I did.

"Unlock the back doors."

"Certainly," I said. "Is there something wrong—?"

Oh, was that a mistake! Never ask if there's something wrong! That means you think there is something wrong!

I could feel Carlos' eyes burning into the back of my head.

"You tell me," the officer said.

I smiled and pushed down the button that unlocked all the doors.

The officer went to the back and opened the two rear doors. He stood there. Looking. He put his hands down on the edge of van and leaned in. He looked with fearsomely cutting eyes at every inch of the back.

He ran his hand over the floor boards. His fingers—his fingers seemed to be rubbing the screw heads.

I looked at him through the rear-view mirror.

I couldn't see perfectly.

But I felt like my stomach was swallowing my heart.

Then he pressed down on the rear bumper and pulled himself up and clamored into the back of the van.

"Good morning, officer," Marisol said turning to him. "Can I help you with anything?"

"Do you know any drug smugglers?" he asked.

"No," Marisol answered.

"Anyone give you anything to bring across the border?"

"No," Marisol answered.

"What about these books?"

"Oh," Marisol said, "those are for the children."

"Which church you teaching at?"

"Our Lady of Lourdes in Campeche. The pastor is Padre Alfonso Madeira."

No one can ever say that Marisol is not a quick study.

"And I speak Spanish," she added, "so I will be the main teacher. I am looking forward to it very much."

"That so?" the guard said.

Then he opened a book. He put it down on the floor and opened another. Then another. Then another.

He opened every single book in the three boxes back there.

Every single one.

"Smugglers—" he said, "they never figure you have the patience to look in every book. They never figure on someone like me."

"Why?" I asked, "would anyone smuggle drugs *into* Mexico?"

"Maybe that's a question you can answer for me, Mr. Missionary from Massachusetts. Do I tell you how to be a missionary?"

"No, officer."

"But you tell me how to do my job?"

"Sorry, officer."

I said nothing further.

"What you people don't think that we know," he said, glaring at me, "is that to smuggle drugs *out* of Mexico you first have to smuggle something *into* Mexico. Know what that something might be?"

I said nothing. I shook my head no.

"They don't give away drugs for nothing," he said.

He started singing a stupid part of a stupid little song.

"Money makes the world go round—"

He kicked a few of the books as he sang, and then he jumped out of the back of the van.

By now, eight more cars had piled up behind us. The line was forming to get into Mexico.

The guard seemed bothered by this.

He walked up to my window and said, "License."

I gave him my license.

"This is a Massachusetts license."

"Yes," I replied.

"Do you have a Texas license?"

"Um. No, officer, I don't."

"Do you have a Mexican license?"

"No, officer, I don't."

"Do you have an international license?"

"No, officer—"

"I can't see how I can let you drive this vehicle into Mexico without a proper license. If you had a Texas license that would be okay. Reciprocity. But you ain't got a Texas license. Or a Mexican license. Or an international license. I can't let you drive this vehicle into Mexico without the proper license."

There was no point in arguing with this man.

He was a small man with a big gun and there was no way in hell that we were going to convince him to let us do anything that we wanted to do.

"I suppose—you'll have to turn this here van around and drive back to—Massachusetts. See, this here license of yours, it's legal in Massachusetts. But it sure as hell ain't legal here in the great state of Texas. So—Mr. Missionary man from Massachusetts—it looks like God's work is going to have to wait. Now don't it?"

"I have an international license!" Pearl yelled out.

He looked across me at her.

"What?" I asked her. "What do you mean?"

"I do," Pearl said. "I never told you. It's not the kind of thing that just comes up in conversation. I've had one for years. My sister and I got them after college. We wanted to go to Paris and drive all over the French countryside. You ever been to France, officer?"

The guard stood motionless.

"Well, neither have I. My sister got pregnant and that was that. One more way she managed to ruin my life. But I had my international driver's license and I keep renewing it every two years. It only costs seventy-five dollars. And it keeps hope alive."

"Show it to me," the guard said.

Pearl opened her pocketbook and took out her wallet and deftly fingered one of the cards and took it out and handed it across me to the officer.

He looked at it. He looked at her.

"Take off you glasses, ma'am."

"Sure," Pearl said, "but please don't call me, 'ma'am.' It makes me sound old."

She took her sunglasses off and looked right at him and smiled and put them right back on.

"I got that red-eye thing. Sharing makeup."

She cast an accusing eye back toward Marisol.

Marisol improvised a shrug, then said, "Everyone blames me."

"The sun hurts my eyes," Pearl continued. "So here I am going to Mexico where there's nothing but sun."

"You drive this vehicle," the officer said. "You're the only one with a license that I can allow to drive it."

"Well—" I began. "Can't I just drive? I mean she has the license. And I'm already at the wheel. And we got all these cars behind us."

"She drives or no one drives. The rest of you get out and go stand in front of that building there. You— The one with the license— You drive across the border there and park in one of those spaces on the Mexico side."

Only he said, "Mee—hee—ko."

I turned around and looked at Carlos, Todd and Marisol.

I was adrift.

We were less than twenty yards from Mexico.

Less than twenty yards from being where we had to be when the vault opened—in seven minutes.

"I need my wrinkle cream," Marisol said, digging through her pocketbook.

"Mom?" Carlos said, his voice full of exasperation. "Now? Wrinkle cream? Now?"

"I need my wrinkle—cream—now more than ever," Marisol answered.

Then Marisol leaned forward just a bit and said, "Pearl, you understand about wrinkles, don't you? Pearl do you know where it is? My wrinkle cream?"

"No," Pearl answered.

"Please look, Pearl. I think I let you borrow it. You may be right about your red-eye condition. I think my wrinkle cream may be in your purse next to your phone. Wrinkle cream. Your phone."

Pearl rummaged through her purse.

"Nothing here."

"Well, maybe it's in my purse," Marisol said. "Maybe it's next to my phone."

"Come on," the guard snapped. "Move it."

The four of us got out of the car and Pearl slid over and sat in the driver's seat.

The guard motioned that we follow him to the small shack. There was a table in front of it and he placed all of our documents on it and seemed to stare at them.

Then he turned to look at the van.

"What the hell is wrong with her?"

He waved to get Pearl's attention.

"Drive!" he shouted.

"She can drive," Marisol said—a little loudly. "She can drive. She's not stupid. All she has to to is turn the key."

The motor started.

"I don't think Pearl has ever driven a van before," Marisol said. "It might take her a minute to figure it out. You know. I mean, the pedals are the same of course. Gas on the right. Brake on the left.

But—the shift is the stick on the right of the wheel and Pearl has never driven a van like that. Her car back home—her Mustang—has the shift on the floor between the seats. It might take Pearl a moment to move the stick down three spaces. These kids. They never drive vans or trucks or do any real work."

Marisol smiled at the guard.

"Are our papers in order?" she asked. "I'm sure they are officer. I'm sure it's—straight. You know. Straight. Very straight."

The van moved slowly forward.

"It is hot already," Marisol said. "But they never listen to me. These young people. You have to drink water. Right? Lots of water. Right? Drink it right now."

The van turned to the right.

"Don't be left in the heat."

"The van turned a bit to the left."

"Stop. Stop with this sun all the time. That's what I say. Stop all this sun."

The van stopped.

Marisol smiled at the officer.

"So many cars today," she said.

He handed her all the papers.

"Walk along that white path there. Rejoin your vehicle. Only she drives."

"Yes, sir," Marisol said.

The door to the guard shack opened and another guard stuck his head out and yelled, "Clarence. Your wife is on the phone again. This time she sounds ugly. Really ugly."

Our guard swore under his breath—and then strode across the little patio and into the shack.

The four of us walked quickly along that white path toward the car.

"Pearl," Marisol shouted as we moved toward the van, "get over to the passenger seat."

"She can't hear you," Carlos said.

"Of course she can. How do you think she drove the van? The only wrinkle, my Carlos, is in my brain."

We were in the van. We were in Mexico. I turned on the engine.

"My God, Pearl," I began to gush, "That was great!"

"Easy," Carlos said. "No emotion until we get away from here."

"Really great," I whispered. "Really, really great!"

And I was driving south.

"What time is it?" Marisol asked.

"It's 9:05," Carlos said.

"Your plan," my Carlos, "was off by two minutes."

"I think that's within statistical limits."

Pearl took her phone out of her purse and hit the "end call" icon.

"Marisol," she said, "it's a good thing you told me about the pedals. I think I could have figured out the shift. But I had no idea about the pedals."

"Can we show emotion now?" I asked.

"Yes," Carlos said, "but drive even and drive straight."

Carlos leaned forward and patted Pearl on the shoulder.

"You are amazing," he said to her. "I couldn't have done it."

Todd and Marisol chimed in, and we band of banditos drove south with happy hearts.

After a minute or two, I turned to Pearl.

"Why in the world," I asked, "do you have an international license?"

"Oh," Pearl said, "that was just a lark. We had graduated high school. Claire and I actually were planning on going to Paris, and she got hers and I got mine too. It's just paperwork. You don't have to drive or anything."

"But don't you have to have an American license first?"

"I did."

"You're blind. You couldn't have a license."

"Really? How did you buy your beer?"

"Oh," I said.

"Oh," Pearl said.

I drove south. Hugging the east coast of Mexico.

We drove for nine more hours. We didn't get any closer than three hundred miles from Campeche and its church and school that would now have no books.

"Remember the hundred thousand dollars," Marisol said.

"I will," I said.

Todd was at the wheel when we pulled up to the border crossing at Belize.

"You know," Carlos said, "we never figured on this part. I mean—we've been assuming they'd let us in since we were coming from Mexico. But—suppose they're really strict? Suppose they make us get out? Suppose they order us to lift up the floor boards?"

"Remember, I can drive if I have to," Pearl said.

Todd stopped the car and lowered the window.

A Belize officer approached the van and spoke to Todd in a crisp British accent.

"Good afternoon, sir."

"Good afternoon, officer."

"What is your purpose entering Belize?"

"We are from the United States. We're here on a missionary trip to Campeche in Mexico. Here are our passports and visas. But—we've heard so much about Belize we thought we'd take a little side trip and take a couple of days off and visit your country."

"I want to see the monkeys," Marisol said, leaning forward in her seat so that the guard would notice her.

"We have many spider monkeys in this part of Belize," he said, smiling at her. If you want to see howler monkeys you'll have to drive much farther south."

"Monkeys is monkeys," Marisol said.

"Actually not," I said. "Actually not at all."

The guard looked over our papers.

"Welcome to Belize," he said. "Enjoy yourselves."

CHAPTER TWENTY-EIGHT
Rain

I remember it looked like rain.

It was May of the following year.

A beautiful sun-drenched day.

A day like all the others in Belize.

Except there was a touch of something in the sky. Rain, I thought. This looks like rain.

I was standing under a shade tree—which is, of course, the national pastime—looking out over our land.

We owned as far as I could see.

That villa that Carlos had found on the internet, back before we robbed the bank, was still for sale when we got to Belize and we bought it. Belize is a really fun place to buy things. All you need is money. We have more than 400 acres with options to purchase more. Carlos likes land. So I'm sure he'll exercise the options and we'll own all that we can see—and a lot that we can't see.

So—how do I catch you up on this story?

Lunch is always a good place to catch up.

Our villa looked out over the ocean, and we had all of our meals—whenever possible—outdoors on the veranda.

Which is exactly what we were doing on this beautiful May afternoon, exactly one year to the day after we robbed the Iron Street Branch of the Boston United Savings Bank and got away with thirty-nine million dollars.

Exactly thirty-nine million dollars.

Carlos was happy with that.

As for the money itself, we were in Belize and could pretty much wave American hundred-dollar bills around with impunity. But thirty-nine million—well, that's a lot of American hundred-dollar bills.

While Marisol was teaching children to read, and while Pearl and I were setting up the clinic, Carlos and Todd came up with a plan to—shall we say—sanitize the money.

We had already changed our names. It was easy to buy passports and birth certificates and whatever else we needed in Belize. We were now the D'Oro family—which is Italian for "golden." We were now originally from the Italian town of Como, on the Swiss border. This would account for both Marisol and Carlos' skin and for my and Todd's blond hair. And Pearl just sort of fit into the middle somewhere. We presented Marisol as our aunt and Carlos as our cousin—so all of us had the same last name. Which made things easier to remember. We kept our first names because we were afraid we'd slip up and, besides, if anyone figured that out they'd figure out the whole thing anyway. Oh—Pearl's

175

maiden name was changed to Saint Claire—a little nod to her sister.

Armed with new names and documents, Carlos and Todd drove up to Belize City and walked into the Belgian National Bank and calmly opened an account with a deposit of thirty million dollars. Carlos did a bunch of things and the next thing we knew was that Carlos and Todd were now licensed traders on the international market—backed by a letter of credit from the Belgian National Bank.

Doing research that would have made both Headmaster Winn and Professor Duncan quite proud, they soon perfected an investment strategy that was as simple as it was profound. After they opened an international online trading account, they built a high-speed computer program that could basically do two things: analyze weather conditions all around the world—and do it with amazing speed and accuracy.

Two much snow in Detroit? The price of rock salt will go up.

Not enough rain in Iowa? Corn prices rise.

Too much rain in India? People need sandbags.

With this program, they could confidently buy and sell any variety of commodities. And they could buy and sell it so quickly—sometimes within seconds—that their profits mounted and mounted. Most of the time, the margins were quite small. Sandbag sacks, for example, could be bought and sold within the same minute at a profit of only two cents per thousand bags.

Buy ten million bags—then sell ten million bags thirty seconds later.

You get the idea.

Money was coming in. Money was going out. The more it moved in and the more it moved out—the cleaner it got.

They were like kids with a new toy.

The money?

Quietly. Behind the scenes. The money moved around Belize.

First, there was enough medical equipment for our clinic.

Then there was enough medical equipment for every clinic and hospital in Belize.

Then there was a fellowship program for Belize students to study medicine in the United States and in Europe. And when they returned to be doctors in their own country, more students would follow suit.

Then every school had books. And computers. And field trips. And visiting artists.

Parks. Community centers. Food banks.

All of it quietly. All of it anonymously. All of it heartfelt.

We easily could have done all that with the original thirty-nine million. But now, with the boys' investments and with trusts and deeds and bequests, we could do it for the rest of time.

Plus—it gave the boys something to do.

I never said this out loud, but I knew that if we were indeed ever arrested—we could convince Belize not to extradite us. We'd promise to pay back the whole 39 million—and we'd promise to keep the trusts intact and provide for Belize for all the years to come. We'd have more than enough to live on and we'd give all the rest to our adopted country.

And so, I was content. I never looked over my shoulder. I lived every day trying to do what was good for my patients. And maybe to find a little happiness in the long languid evenings.

And so, we drifted on. Doing what our dreams told us to do.

We were happy.

Carlos had another reason to be very happy. Laura. A beautiful young British woman who worked at the Consulate.

Carlos and his Laura came out to the veranda. Holding hands, they took their seats at the table, with the wide blue Caribbean stretching out before them.

I walked over and joined them. I sat and puffed on a cigar—a Cohiba as I had predicted.

Todd came out of the house and lit up a Cohiba of his own and sat at the table.

We were very fond of Cohibas—but, and this seemed strange coming from Marisol, we were forbidden to smoke inside.

"I hope you boys don't think of this as losing your—autonomy?" Marisol had said the first day we tried to light up.

"No, Mom," I answered dutifully. "Carlos and I will only smoke outside."

Anyway, getting back to our lunch, we talked for a bit about maybe going sailing later in the day in our 1981 38-foot Catalina sailing boat that we had recently bought. It was built for racing. But we preferred quiet peaceful trips just offshore. Keeping the shore in sight, might have had something to do with Mom and Dad. More probably, we simply had no desire to explore the ocean. We had one new world to live in, and that was quite enough.

We talked a bit about maybe having dinner in town for a change.

We talked about the need to get some more exercise—maybe starting next week.

We talked and we talked.

We talked a bit about all manner of this and that.

Then Todd made an announcement.

"I met a girl today," Double-D said. "I like her a lot. She works at that little hut of a restaurant in the village. Her family runs it. I got some coffee. We got to talking."

"What's her name?" I asked.

"Maria. She's Belizean. She's Mayan."

"You should have invited her over."

"I did," Todd said, "she should be here any minute."

Then there was Marisol, who came out of the villa carrying a tray of paella and sat at our table. We got paella when she was very happy—or when we had to get serious. This was a happy paella.

Marisol was Headmistress of the New Beginnings Academy. It turned out that Marisol had indeed a penchant for teaching. She came alive more than ever for the children. She talked to them. She sang to them. She played games with them. They loved her and she loved them back.

Marisol unfolded a copy of the *Boston Globe* that was two days old, but new to us.

"It's still going on," she said.

We hadn't known it at the time, of course, but as we were driving toward Belize after crossing into Mexico, two Carlisle squad cars pulled up at Shel Crummins' mansion and found the van and then found the money.

That and the text message to the Carlisle Police Department set a lot of things in motion. The newspapers were in a tizzy. The police were under scrutiny. The FBI wanted answers.

Then the whole case was turned over to the U.S. Attorney's office. State lines had been crossed. The money had come from the Federal Reserve. Local and state officials sighed in relief—this troublesome case was out of their hands and the Feds were welcome to it.

Shel Crummins, Clive Williams, Jonathan Slocum and Mario Mollacare weren't indicted for anything as of yet—but their lives were in a fish bowl and their lawyers' fees were fast approaching becoming a stack of hundred-dollar bills at least nine feet tall.

Meanwhile, Marisol learned a few things from Reverend DuValle—as she and the pastor of the Church of Divine Faith still conversed, only now on pre-paid cell phones that could not be traced.

The Church of Our Lady of Lourdes in Campeche had indeed received an anonymous gift of $100,000—which they were using to build new classrooms and buy books and hire teachers.

"Isn't that the turn of events that is nice?" Marisol asked.

"And," Reverend DuValle continued, "your former house on Beacon Hill was donated to us. It was given to us. For free."

"Another nice turn," Marisol said.

"Do you know about this?" the reverend asked.

"All I know," Marisol said, "is that God works in not-so-mysterious ways."

The reverend knew that the better part of good fortune is found in silence—and he asked no more questions.

"But," Marisol said to us, "he did give me some interesting news."

When the Alonzos showed up in court to claim our company, a very strange thing occurred. The magistrate said everything was in good order. The Alonzos burst into wild applause—but Juanita burst into tears. Questioned by her cohorts, she said that it wasn't right that we had lost our company. Sure, she fell. But it was a simple accident on her part. We were not to blame at all. She cried out to the magistrate from her wheelchair that they didn't deserve to own the company. Her husband Hermann and her brother Luis tried to silence her.

"I will not be quiet!" she apparently screamed in court. "I will not be quiet. I have been quiet too long. Yes, I was hurt. Yes, I will never walk again. But it was an accident. People told us to sue. People told us to get all the money we could get! It is too much. We must pay some of it back."

So, to the astounded Alonzo clan, Juanita made a vow that they would deposit five hundred dollars a week from now on into my savings account at Boston United Savings Bank.

"For how long?" Hermann asked his wife.

"For until I say to stop!" she screamed.

And that's what they have been doing. And that's what they will continue to do, as long as Juanita has her way.

The magistrate asked a few questions about the "people" Juanita had alluded to. Juanita snapped back to her senses—more or less—and said it was just family members. The magistrate had one of those brain leaps and asked if it had been anyone in the employ of the Boston United Savings Bank. Juanita clutched for a moment. Then she said that, no, it was her family.

That momentary clutch was enough for the magistrate to contact the FBI and add another little wrinkle to the case.

"The police will never figure out this mess," Marisol said. "I love reading about it. I love talking to Reverend Father Phillippe about it. It makes me happy to think that the bastardos have been stopped. What do you think they will do?"

"They'll screw it up," I answered. "I have faith in their ability to screw it up."

Just then Maria walked out onto the veranda.

Todd introduced her to all of us.

"You're the doctor?" she said to me. "At the clinic?"

"Yes," I said. "I'm Dr. Timothy D'Oro."

Wow, that felt so good.

"But please call me, Tim."

"My little sister came to your clinic last month," Maria said. "We were very worried. We thought it was her brain."

"Oh, I remember her," I said. "No. It was just a bad sinus infection. How is she doing?"

"All better. Thanks to you."

"Glad to be able to help."

"And your nurse who sat at the front desk—the very attractive woman who is blind—she was so wonderful afterwards," Maria said.

"That's nice to hear. She's also my wife. Oh. Here she is now."

At that moment, Pearl came out of the villa and stepped onto the veranda.

"Pearl," I called, "we have two guests. You know Laura of course. And this is Maria."

Pearl took off her sunglasses. She looked right at me. And she smiled. Then she walked across the veranda, sidestepping a few chairs along her path with ease. She said hello to Marisol and to Carlos and Laura and to Todd.

She approached Maria.

"Maria," she said, holding out her hand, "so nice to meet you."

"We've met," Maria said. "At the clinic last month. You were the one who was so nice to my little—"

Maria stopped talking. She couldn't help staring at Pearl.

Pearl smiled. She was used to it by now.

Pearl's eyes were still as beautiful as ever. But they were no longer blue.

Pearl had the bright yellow eyes of the simian.

"It turns out," I said by way of explanation, "that Howler monkeys have eyes that are very compatible with human eyes."

I looked at Pearl carefully.

"The swelling is completely gone," I said.

"I feel great," Pearl answered. "No double vision at all."

"You— You did the operation?" Maria asked.

"Yes. Here in our clinic."

"Could you— Could you do the same for children?"

"We already have a little boy who we think would be a perfect candidate," I answered.

"Marisol, look!" Pearl yelled.

"That is no longer funny, my Pearl."

"No, look. Out over the ocean. A rainbow."

There was indeed a rainbow.

Marisol put her hand to her mouth, as if to stifle a cry.

"When I see a rainbow," she said, "I think that it is sent from my little Martinez. Telling me not to worry."

We were silent. I think we would have remained silent for some time, thinking, I suppose, of rain and snow and sun—and life.

But it started to rain.

The others squealed and happily dashed for indoors—protecting the paella as they ran.

I moved to follow them, but Pearl grabbed my arm to hold me back.

"We'll get wet," I said.

"Who's cares?" she said. "I want to get wet with you."

I leaned forward and kissed her and took her in my arms.

"I love your eyes," I said,

"Thank you for giving them to me," she said and kissed me.

She leaned up and whispered something in my ear.

"Oh, my God!" I cried out. "Pearl—that is so wonderful!"

"Do you want a boy or a girl?"

I held her tightly and answered, "I don't care if it's a boy or a girl. As long as he or she has your strength."

"I love my bandit," Pearl said and kissed me like she was conducting an opera.

"I have never been so happy," I said. "I love to think that every morning I will wake up lying next to you."

She flashed those perfectly beautiful eyes and we scampered into the house to tell everyone the great news—when Todd reminded us that twins run in the family.

Lloyd Gordon lives in Boston, Massachusetts, with his wife, Diane. He is semiretired, having owned a national plastics-manufacturing company that he sold in 2000, and he still oversees a large industrial real-estate enterprise in the Pittsburgh area. An avid golfer, he is continuously on a quest for the perfect swing, but he settles for finding his golf ball. Lloyd and Diane's major joy comes from their children and grandchildren.

Made in the USA
Charleston, SC
27 July 2014